Chicago Jihad

Fiction

PrivatePress

Chicago Jihad

Copyright © 2022 Garry A. Hamud
Garry A. Hamud, aka, G.A. Hammad, Author

All Rights Reserved, including the right of reproduction in whole or in part in any form whatsoever.

For information regarding special discounts for bulk purposes and education, please contact __author@chicagojihad.com__ on a confidential basis.

http://chicagojihad.com

Manufactured in the United States of America

Library of Congress Control Number: 2022907100

International Standard Book Number: 978-0-5-78-28691-4

To David, RIP

PrivatePress

Chicago Jihad

Chapter 1

Hamid Karzai International Airport, The Escape

Hot as hell, stench of sewage, deafening mass of desperate humanity, all at Abbey Gate, to get out of Kabul, what idiot ordered this, explosions front and center, find Ramin, Captain in what's left of the Afghan army, dirty, exhausted, pissed off, screaming into his mic, "Rashid, come in, abort Abbey Gate, go to East Gate, everyone NOW, we are under ISIS attack, repeat, East Gate, will see you there, inish Allah."

Nothing to defend, no hope, it's all about survival for Ramin and his family, wife, Tamara, one little boy, Jamil – just eight years old, his younger brother, Rashid, a warrior himself, educated, interpreter for the Allies, all trying desperately to escape the hell hole of Kabul, Rashid's wife too, Aslan, a modern Moslem woman, their two little girls, Magi and Mona. "Where will this all end," he wonders aloud.

Ramin's radio crackles. "Yes, of course," he says, "bring Hamid too and his wife, Yasmine, we will make room." A young married couple, friends, lost their own child to kidnapping last year, never found, maybe now a child wife. Ramin vomits at the idea.

Sounds of RPGs, AKs, and AR 15s fill the air, chaos, finally, Ramin hears Blackhawks overhead to settle up the matter. Why so long to get here, Ramin wonders, now nearly at the East Gate himself, to wait.

Ramin checks his ammo, two clips, he's locked and loaded, pausing just a second to look at his ring, names engraved in it, a gift from his late mother, killed by the Taliban, Ramin, Warrior, Rashid, Rightly Guided, God willing, she was right.

Security at the East Gate is heavy, less civilians, more soldiers, Afghan regulars and U.K. Marines. "Salaam brothers," a wave from Ramin to subordinates, he turns to look out in anguish for eight of his family and friends he prays to somehow safely deliver to sanctuary and freedom in United States. Every minute counts, there is but one hour left to catch a ride out on a U.S. Air Force C 17.

"Ramin, come in, it's Rashid, we are here, where are you?" a click on a button tells him to meet at west side flag pole, no flag flying, where Ramin is standing on a bench, waiting the group. "You made it, Allah Akbar, did you bring the bag?"

Rashid could barely hear him. "Yes I brought it, but Taliban took it at the last checkpoint," meaning everything of value they had was gone for good. "They did give us bread and water," says Tamara, while she and the children piled on and hugged him.

"OK, OK," said Ramin, "Let me breathe already," laughing slightly for one last time in what is now the arm pit of the world.

"It is arranged, everything is paid, we go now, all of us, no stopping, direct to that plane," Ramin pointing to an Air Force C 17 surrounded by a mob, just 300 meters through the gate. "If we get separated just remember we can connect through friends at the Freedom Mosque on East 51st Street, Chicago, Illinois, in the great U.S.A. Now, Go, Go, Go."

Ramin is last to move out, gives his gear and rifle to security on the way. Inish Allah, all will be well.

East Gate is now sealed behind Ramin, the C 17 can carry 650, looks to him like room for all. His family and friends are nowhere in sight; no radio, nothing, just the clothing on his back. Ramin is next to last on board, safely in the hands of the United States Air Force, no idea what the next stop will be.

The sun is just setting on this clear and hot day. The family's last day home, when the monster plane goes airborne, no windows, nothing electronic. All cell phones, watches, you name it, taken by the Taliban. Few had any idea of time.

Crew orders over the Public Address, "Sit up, sit still, and be silent. Rest." Everyone obeyed. Collapse might be a better word, thought Ramin. He knew the hour, could feel a steep climb angle over the mountains of his native land. Banking to the South, he figured this was a jump flight to a close in base for fuel, food, and chance to meet up with his family before the long journey half way around the globe.

Sure enough, another Crew Alert, "Remain seated for the duration of the flight, we land in 15 minutes, on the ground, you will, ONE, exit to the rear; TWO, form into ranks at the instruction of ground personnel; THREE, process identification clearances; FOUR, receive a personal hygiene kit for full bathroom break; FIVE, have a hot meal in the cafeteria before; SIX, departure at 900 hours. All is mandatory, repeat mandatory, including for women and children. No exceptions."

Ramin, at the rear of the cargo compartment, felt the smooth landing, heard the sound of the giant engines winding down, watched lights come on and exit ramp deploy. At an instant the Crew personnel appeared. "You," pointing at Ramin, "move it, everyone follow that man, Go, Go, Go," and a sea of over 600 souls moved in synch out and to the ground, greeted by ground personnel, barking commands, effecting the plan as described.

Ramin could see everyone coming off the plane, there they were, wife, Tamara, brother Rashid, everyone. They looked exhausted, worried, all together, in rank, going through the motions, on their way to liberation, or so they hoped. When they saw Ramin, everyone was overjoyed.

Rashid grabbed Ramin, and everyone joined into a tight group hug. Hamid and Yasmine too. Hamid repeating, "Thank you, thank you both for our lives," and "thanks to Allah too, especially to Allah. Allah Akbar." (translation God is Great)

Food was hot. No pork, chicken, rice, lima beans, lots of gravy, hot tea, and a Hostess Cup Cake – so different to them, so delicious, among friends. Rashid reminded them, "All from their American saviors, Allah Akbar." Everyone repeated it, more than once.

"I hope you found the food satisfactory, the gift of the American taxpayer," said a large man in military garb at the front of the room.

"My name is Captain Ruger. You are under Military Control. Later on, when the civilians take command, it will be the Federal law of the United States of America as your destination."

"In the United States, all people believe, no matter race, creed, color, gender, religion that everyone is born equal, and you better believe that too. Likewise, it is unlawful to strike another person, especially a man hitting a woman or child – that is illegal and cowardly, we do not accept it. I saw a man strike a person I now know to be his wife, and he knows who I am talking about – I will tell you all once – learn this lesson, stop it, or go home. I hate cowardly men."

"You are all now dismissed to prepare to board your plane when you hear your orders over the Public Address."

The room buzzed with conversation, and Ramin gave a thumbs up to everyone in his group – they were all smiles.

Chapter 2

The getting off plane drill was repeated getting back onboard. This time, the women insisted they sit next to their men, friends and children all around. Gratitude, relief, hope was in the air, so was the plane for 10 hours 20 minutes, until touch down. This time in Guam, for a repeat of the same routine – fresh clothing and new Identification Cards in English. Ice cream for the children, Jamil, Magi, and Mona, and, as this was a new land, no separation of boys and girls, men and women. Everyone was together, and Aslan, Tamara and Yasmine all agreed. "This is the right way to live," said Yasmine to all.

By late afternoon, three aircraft and civilians, were ready for takeoff. The lone 757 on the tarmac held Ramin's entire group of weary travelers. Rashid, using his language skills, had learned the itinerary. He told the assembly, "After takeoff, a rest stop for fuel in Los Angeles, then, on to Chicago O-Hare, about 24 hours travel all tolled."

Aslan, the school teacher back home, chimed in. "Meaning we hope to arrive in Chicago in the early morning, right, figure some delays, that would be perfect."

"Any arrival as far as I am concerned is perfect, God willing," says Yasmine.

Agreed, except Jamil liked Guam – the people, the island, and he loved the ice cream. He had never eaten ice cream. "I want to stay here," he was heard to complain just before takeoff.

Ramin thought to himself, never doubt a child. He told his wife Tamara, "You know, Jamil may be right. I am worried. I am for the first time in years unarmed." Tamara laughed, her first laugh in a long time. "Don't be nervous, you don't need a gun in

Chicago, America, and you have me by your side," her beautiful eyes twinkled above her mask.

Everyone had beautiful eyes in Afghanistan. Everyone wore masks. They all thought this was just like back home, figuring the mask requirement would never go away.

Flying high over the Pacific, a beverage, no alcohol, a restless sleep for all after years of war and insecurity. Loss of everything, including their country, in what was a shameful surrender before the world that cut deeply into the hearts of the men who had fought so hard, like Ramin and Rashid. RIP all the dead.

Ramin, filled with the worry of what was yet to come, hoped for God's favor.

No disembarkation in Los Angeles, lights around the plane light the cloudy sky, soon enough, gassed up, ready for takeoff, to the new world ahead.

The plane backed out of the gate. "You know Ramin, you and Rashid have flown before but not us," said Tamara, "All this is so new." Aslan chimed in, "Yes, true, and this airplane, I love to fly in it. This is truly the new world, oh my God."

Everyone in earshot agreed, their faces said it all.

As the plane climbed out of LAX, over the Pacific, banking to the north, heading northeast, everyone could see the expanse of what is known as LA, "Amazing, unimaginable. Oh my God, the city is as big as 100 of our country – what is this USA?"

Exclamations from row after row of the weary travelers. Hamid and Yasmine peered out the windows, so excited and in disbelief. Hamid heard to repeat time and time again, "thanks to God, this is our new home, Chicago cannot be so big."

"We shall soon find out," echoed Ramin, "Inish Allah."

One hour before arrival, a woman stood up in the front of the plane, "I'm Officer Mary Bell, the U.S. Department of State Officer in Charge. In Chicago, she explained, you will be cleared by U.S. Customs and Border Patrol, and the local Covid Task Force, including testing for everyone. Then, to a secondary inspection by the Immigration Service, including specially trained asylum Agents. Background and Biometrics will be done, including pictures and fingerprints. No religious objections allowed, this is a security matter and 100% mandatory. Everyone admitted will be classified as a Refugee. All forms will be done at the point of entry. Once approved, you get indefinite stay status and work authority, all at once. Any questions?"

None.

Officer Bell was followed by someone from Health and Human Services. He said, no name given, "Thank you, Officer Bell. Furthermore, before you leave the airport in Chicago, and transport has been arranged to take you to your temporary lodgings where you can stay for up to five days to acclimate, the Department, along with local non-profits, will provide you with everything you will need to make a new life in Chicago. Meaning a stipend of $500.00 cash, a Federal Identification Card, a prepaid Credit Card with $1,500 for food and clothing as needed, your physical address, and a voucher for transport to your new digs. Don't lose your Credit Card, it will be recharged on a monthly basis in an amount to be determined on inspection and arrival. Meals will be prepared for you at your temporary lodgings. Any questions?"

None, just a mix of voices saying, "Thank you," in various dialects.

"Thank you, Thank America." Aslan smiled at Rashid, everyone saw, they held hands, hope was in the air.

Cruising altitude, clouds below partially blocked the view of the vastness of the United States. Some pulled away from the windows, all in disbelief of what they had seen. Ramin, one of the few not smiling, said to his wife and the others, "How in the world did this country, these people, surrender to the Taliban, who cannot even read nor write. How can it be?" he said, feeling the pain and humiliation of the defeat and evacuation.

There was no answer, but everyone wondered too.

Ramin spoke again, to everyone in earshot, "I have been with the Americans in battle. They are brave, they are decent. You can see how we are treated. We should always express our thanks."

"Agreed," was the reply, from everyone.

"How should we live in Chicago; it will be different?" asked Aslan.

This time Rashid replied, "From now on, you can pray 5 times a day, but to yourself. The Koran allows this in places not familiar. You may have to eat food not halal, but no pork. Be careful and understand that women and children are equals. They go to school and they can go out without a man escort. They can even work."

Rashid went on, "Women can still cover their heads, and the COVID mask orders are good, all covering faces. No burkas – do not call such attention, just cover skin and be modest."

Everyone agreed and the girls were happy with the outcome. "Great, we can do this, it might be fun too." With that Rashid looked at Aslan and the others and smiled, "This was indeed a new world."

Disbelief grew the farther and longer the plane flew over the mighty, beautiful heartland of the USA. Amazement hardly describes the feeling throughout the passenger compartment. "How did this great nation fall on its knees before the hated Taliban, how, only Allah knows," one unknown person said it, repeated by others.

Chapter 3

"Cabin, prepare for landing in Chicago," the Pilot's voice rang through the cabin. Ramin, Rashid and the others were awake, peering out of windows at the expanse of lakes and the City of Chicago.

"My God, what is this, Rashid?" said Hamid. "This is bigger than Los Angeles. Oh my God."

It all seemed infinite. Rashid answered, "They are nearly the same yet smaller than New York." People in earshot were speechless.

After landing, things happened fast. Everyone was taken to a greeting hall and divided into groups. The processing began with COVID tests, fingerprints, photographs for Biometrics, identification, questions to answer – written and verbal, one person at a time.

No announcement, everyone knew this process would take most of the evening.

"Do I go talk by myself, Daddy," Jamil asked. The answer to him and all the children from Aslan was, "Yes, they want to know from you who is your family – your father, mother and siblings. Do not be afraid."

Ramin was taken out of the group. Tamara asked him, "Is it because you are military?" Ramin had no idea.

"Ramin, how many people are you traveling with?" asked an Officer in a blue uniform, military grit. Answer, "six adults, three children, all family."

With that, Ramin was seated. He was informed, "Ramin, your group is in Group 1 and will be processed first then going to temporary housing at the LaQuinta Chicago for five days with all expenses, including food, paid. It's nice there. Thank you for your five years of service – we don't forget it."

Ramin smiled. "Thank you, brother."

"You are most welcome. Here is your Federal Identification, stipend of $500.00 cash, and your Credit Card. It is like money, you understand, $1,500.00 prepaid. Your LaQuinta Chicago room reservations are for three rooms, three families."

"Yes, Sir, thank you very much," Ramin said.

"OK, you are leader of your group. When they all have their papers, move through that security check point, clear the gates, and take Bus 1 to your destination. Welcome to the United States of America."

That was so kind, Ramin thought to himself, as he waited to be joined by the others. They came, wife, Tamara, with Jamil, followed by brother, Rashid, with Aslan, Magi and Mona, followed by Hamid and Yasmine.

"This place is so big for an airport. It is a city, oh my God, and the Americans are so pleasant to us. I am very happy," Aslan said to everyone. All were nearly speechless and in awe.

"Where do we go?" asked Rashid. "Follow me," answered Ramin. "We go to Bus 1 through there, to the LaQuinta Chicago Hotel for five days, then we will settle in our new digs, we learn about later."

Once outside on the sidewalk – cold, dark, so busy, cars, buses, people everywhere carrying small parcels of personal items. "Scary feeling, like our feet are not touching ground. So different – loud, fast, like the scurry of battle, true?" asked Ramin.

"Yes," said Tamara. "It is happiness and fear of the unknown all in one. We all feel it."

Dozens of other refugees could be seen from inside Bus 1, coming and going, like in circles. Soon, Bus 1 was full and on the way, one hour Estimated Arrival Time (ETA) to LaQuinta, a shower, clean bed, and rest. Inish Allah.

Everyone had a window seat. Voices of the travelers never stopped. "So big the streets. Oh my God, so many cars and so many people. What is this, all these tall buildings?"

"I am happy, I am scared and this is unimaginable," said Aslan. Others chimed in, "Me Too."

The hotel was beautiful.

"This is the most beautiful building I have ever been inside," said Yasmine.

"It is our home for five days," answered Hamid. A special table was set up with the sign, Welcome Afghan Refugees. On the table were prepared packages, one for each family, with a room number, key, maps, masks, and hand sanitizer. A gentleman at the table gave out the packages and put green wrist bands on everyone. He said, "Please don't take them off, they are your identification in the Hotel for security and dining. Enjoy your stay."

He went on, "like the others, you will need some clothing. There is a Goodwill Store across the street. Everything is clean and fresh, just not new and very inexpensive – you can maybe start there."

"Yes, thank you," answered Hamid and Rashid, in unison.

"Shopping," Aslan said. The girls and the children all heard this and smiled.

A Note in the package provided more detail:

In the Dining Room

Breakfast at 6:00 a.m. to 9:00 a.m.

Lunch at 1:00 p.m.

Dinner at 7:00 p.m.

No Exceptions

Coffee and Tea 24/7 in the Lobby

Valid for Each Person for Five Days

Show Your Wrist Band for Entry

Welcome!

Everyone was on the 8th Floor in adjoining rooms. They took the elevator to get there. While waiting for the lift, Tamara listened to Magi, "I have never been in an elevator." "Me neither," said her sister, Mona, and the same for Jamil.

The children rattled on until the lift arrived. Off they all went to the 8th floor.

With so many rooms, Tamara wondered where to go until hearing Ramin's voice, "This way, follow me." Soon everyone filed into their rooms, clean and bright with big windows and best bathrooms ever seen. All were tired, giving prayerful thanks to Allah, then followed by showers being exhausted and excited. "We are safe now," said Ramin.

"Thanks to God," answered Tamara. Magi and Mona giggled, a happy nervous giggle, feeling no fear, just relief, and in warm bed to sleep.

Ramin told everyone, "Tomorrow, up at 5:00 a.m. for prayers in the room and then breakfast. Wear clean cloths, OK Tamara. We can wash the rest at the end of the hall. The Americans even gave us machine tokens. Bless the Americans. Good night, all."

Lights out.

Chapter 4

Magi, Mona and Jamil were first into the dining room, never had they seen such a breakfast. "This is a blessing from Allah, let us sit and eat what has been given," said Tamara. And everyone did just that.

After breakfast they went shopping for clothing across the street. "How exciting. How much time do we have and what do we do?" asked Tamara.

Ramin answered, "This is a new experience for you, I know. So, like on the Base back home, use the cart, collect what you like, take your time, and we pay when we leave at the cashier."

That said, everyone was off and running.

It was not long before the carts were full, shirts, jackets, pants, even socks, and underwear for the men and boy. Also some nice long dresses and sweaters for the women and children. Scarves too, modest and nice.

"I think this will be OK with our husbands. Do you think so?" asked Tamara to the others. After some back and forth, it was agreed. "Yes, this is modest if we can make it work," answered Aslan. Yasmine smiled in agreement.

"Let's see what you men have found," said Aslan. "Oh, Rashid, how handsome you will look in these new things," eliciting smiles and thanks from everyone.

It was a good shopping day. Total price paid by Ramin on his card was $286.

Back at the hotel it was soon to be lunch. Jamil announced, "Oh great, Mommy, it's going to be Hamburgers. I cannot wait, a real American hamburger and Coca Cola."

Before lunch it was fashion show time to share what was bought. "Jamil, can you show us your new things?" asked Tamara. Everyone gathered around to give some attention to little Jamil. The show started with smiles and laughter all around.

Lunch was as promised. "This is now my favorite food on earth, the American Hamburger, no, Cheeseburger. It is so good," Jamil said to everyone that could hear. Magi and Mona agreed.

Hamid, with hamburger in hand said, "Thanks to God for the Americans. God Bless our friends and family back home, inish Allah. All will be better for everyone."

The welcome package included a coupon for Z Mobile for 9 cell phones and a family plan, prepaid by the government for one year. After lunch all were off to Z Mobile for smartphones.

"Children, please sit down on the bench with us. Your father will get all matters arranged for us," said Aslan. LG G6 cells for everyone. Nice. Thus causing Ramin to comment, "by the grace of God, and the Americans, we can all stay in touch, even with back home, with these phones."

"Yes, we must go to our rooms to study how to use the magic device," Aslan said. Everyone chuckled. The rest of the afternoon was all about cell phones.

Time past and cells were working. Everyone had the same apps and contacts. Ramin and Rashid had the news sites. Everyone had a good translator on the phone too, going back and forth between English and Afghan.

"Get your news set up on your phones, Fox is best," said Ramin. "Tomorrow we go recon our locale and study the lay of the land. In the afternoon, the man comes with our housing plans."

Bed time, lights out.

Chapter 5

Next morning, the men met in the lobby, Ramin was already waiting. "We go first across the street to buy those pocket knives in the case, one for each. No way we walk around naked." Total price was $24.00. Ramin handed one to each man, Hamid accepted his pocket knife, still looking down into the glass showcase.

"Ramin, get this. It is a map book of Chicago. It's only $5.00."

With that done, the three men left the store. They could all see a skyscraper to the south like nothing they had ever imagined. The Willis Tower, it said on the map Hamid held, "OK, we go south."

Everything was nice, clean – another world. Rashid was taking notice of the streets as they walked. "Men, these streets, they are names of U.S. Presidents. You see here, Monroe, Adams, now Jackson." If anyone would know, it was Rashid. "We cannot go too far today. Let us turn east here, toward the big lake."

Ramin was looking more at people than places. "So many different kinds of people, men and women, walking fast and alone, black, brown, white, even Chinese. All very different and new to the Afghans."

"There is the lake. Look a beautiful park too, so big," Rashid said. Now with the map, he said, "they call it Millennium Park." They all stopped to admire its vastness. "Look too, a playground for children. Jamil and the girls will love it, this Maggie Daley Park."

"Especially Magi," chimed in Ramin, "It is named after her,

tomorrow after breakfast, we all come here - everyone deserves a break, this will be it."

Rashid replied, "Inish Allah, thanks to God, the weather is nice and the women and children will be so happy. Let's start back. We have news to share."

A quick turn to the west, all seemed to know the way. With old instincts intact, they were soon back to LaQuinta.

Ramin wanted Rashid to learn everything about Chicago from phones and the map book. "OK, Ramin, work in progress."

Just off the elevator, all three were rushed by their wives and children, all buzzing with excitement. "What did you see, where did you go?", the children pulling on their sleeves – all of them.

Ramin was in the lead, "OK, everyone come in our room. Let us share the news of our small discoveries." Tamara smiled back and reached for her husband's hand.

There was not much time before lunch. The story got told and everyone was excited to hear about Maggie Daley Park. Aslan jumped in first, "We will go after breakfast, inish Allah, and we will take some food and drinks with us so we can enjoy the whole of the day."

The plans were made. Tamara and Yasmine had their own ideas to share. "This is so nice. Thank you, my dear husband," said Tamara. The other women repeated the same words with smiles and hugs all around. A sense of relief of being home again.

Lunch was spaghetti and beef meatballs. Hamid got the last plate. "Well, it's not rice, but it is from the Americans and from God, so we are thankful." There was ice cream dessert, and, of course, tea for everyone.

"Cell phones," stated Aslan, before leaving the table, "Children, you have all our Contacts and the Location is on. WhatzApp is on so we can talk, but no social media or music."

"Let's test our phones by texting and calling each other. Then, let's go upstairs to wait for the man about our new home."

It was not long before the room phone rang. Mr. Everett, from the government said, "please come down to the breakfast room to see me about your new homes and jobs."

It was decided Aslan and Tamara would go with the men to learn about their future.

Mr. Everett was waiting downstairs. "Hello all. Welcome to the United States. I hope everything is satisfactory for you."

I am Ramin, bumped elbows with him, "Yes, thank you. This is my brother, Rashid, his wife Aslan, and my wife Tamara and my dear friend Hamid. Hamid's wife, Yasmine, remains upstairs with the children."

Mr. Everett said, "Please do sit down." He was handing out papers and a map to everyone. "This will be your new address on Halsted Street, to the south. Each family has one apartment. They are adjoining, so you will all be close, on the 2nd floor. It is more secure than the first floor."

"Yes, Mr. Everett, the pictures and everything looks very pleasant. Thank you," Aslan said.

Mr. Everett said, "Well, it is for one year the rent is paid, as is the electricity and gas. All in your names, as you are the sublessee. Please all sign here," gesturing to a lease document for all to sign.

He went on, "There is a Mosque close by, the Twhead. It is walking distance and there is public transport close, right in front of your homes. When you get a car, there is parking as well. The units have heating and cooling, so you will be safe at home and comfortable."

"Schools?" asked Aslan. He replied, "Yes, the children will all go to Elgin School, two blocks away, across from the Elgin Park. It is all walking distance. The administrators expect you next week. No uniforms for the children, just casual, clean clothing. Everything else, including lunch is provided."

"Lunch too, so very nice, can we go with the children the first day?"

"Yes, Aslan, this is expected. You should walk the children to school and walk them home at the close of school. That would be at 2:30 p.m. All the information is in the school brochure."

"We will read. All will be fine. Thank you, again."

"Jobs. Let's move on. Ramin, with your background you can report any day to Chicago Security, Inc. and interview for your new position as Security Guard, starting on day shift, five days a week with a salary of $22.00 an hour. It has been arranged, unless you later object."

Ramin said, "Very good. Is it armed security?"

"Not yet, you need experience, but that will come with time, and a good raise in pay too but later on."

"Rashid, you may report to the Tribunal Newspaper. Here are your directions and whom to see. You are set to start as an Intern in the Diversity Communities News Section, five days a week, again $22.00 an hour. Your language skills will be helpful. Before you go, please visit the Mosque. Find out more about local ethnic and Moslem news, wants, needs, interests and the like. Foods too, a story, you will finish it."

Aslan jumped in, "How nice, Rashid knows all about food."

"Hamid, as you were a medic in training, you will go to Mercy EMT, to work as an intern / assistant. Go and see them this month. Here are your papers. OK, interview, see what you think and if you can do it. Again $22.00 an hour."

"Thank you, Mr. Everett, I will do my best."

Mr. Everett held out more papers, "These are medical care

cards, Medicaid, so you all have access to medical care 24/7."

"You have the bus schedules too. Work is within five miles of your home, no transfers are required. Pretty easy. Study it, please. There are nine bus passes in your papers too. Don't lose them. You will get new ones every month, one for each person in your group."

"And, ladies, there is shopping close by for food. I see you have your cell phones, so you shall be busy making the homes livable and taking care of family. Later on, who knows, work or school, as you like."

"You have a few more days here, so do try to bus over to your new apartments. Look around, just don't go out at night – it is not safe in the city in most areas."

"Did I miss anything, any questions?" looking at Rashid as he spoke, packing up his other papers.

Rashid stood up, "We will study everything. We are reading the news, watching TV, and we will become familiar. If we have questions, can we call you, yes?"

"Oh yes, so sorry, here is my card. And please put it in all your phones. It is a 24/7 number. If I don't answer, leave a message and call any time. You can text me too. Remember, 911 is the emergency number for police, fire, or ambulance. Do tell the children."

"It's getting late, I must go. Let's talk tomorrow morning by phone to recap and be sure all is well. I forget to mention the apartments are fully furnished and all you need to do is get the keys from the Manager, Ms. Paula Jinx in Apartment No. 1. Her telephone number is in the paperwork."

Everyone by now was standing with Mr. Everett, before another word could be said, he was off. The families stayed downstairs for little while, talking, going over things.

Ramin looked at the group. "We must study every detail, all of us. Recon all the areas and we all learn, inish Allah, all will be well, God willing."

Back to the room, Yasmine opened the door. "I would like to know everything, this is such a big moment."

The hours passing by, the adults sat around the dining room table, reviewed every single word of every document, bus schedule, and maps. They would be prepared for anything, they thought. Ramin, blurry eyed said, "Very well, good night. Time to rest, Allah Maackun."

No dinner this evening since everyone was stuffed from lunch. Milk and cookies were brought in the room for the children and evening prayers were said. Early to bed, a new beginning was upon them.

Before lights out, Ramin's phone rang. "A salaam amalecum. Yes, thank you. We arrived safe. We are here at the LaQuinta. Yes, six of us, with three children. Thank you. Yes, we saw Mr. Everett. Very well, inish Allah, tomorrow."

Before anyone could ask, Ramin announced, "That was Imam Akeem from the Mosque. He said we must visit him one day, all of us, to welcome us, I agreed. We will all go as soon as possible. Let us all sleep now, good night."

"This is wonderful news, to meet the Imam Akeem."

"Yes, Aslan, this is good news – welcome news."

Chapter 6

The next day, very early, everyone was ready for the day out and full of excitement.

Rashid knew most of the staff at breakfast. He greeted the Manager, Reuben, "Good morning to you." The Manager looked away from the TV to greet him.

"Who is that on TV, Reuben?"

"That is Mayor Heavyhand. She is saying she will run for reelection."

"I am excited to announce I am running for reelection, with my wife by my side. Take a bow, dear," motioning to a man in a suit on stage.

"I don't understand Reuben, she called the man her wife. What is this?"

"It is confusing. Mayor Heavyhand was a man, turned into a woman. Maybe you can tell. And when she changed, she took that man as her wife."

Ramin was listening, sort of counting on his fingers, working all this out. "No, that does not work, does it?"

Reuben laughed out loud, "Oh yeah, Mayor Heavyhand changed."

"XRSTV, Jack Smith. What about the skyrocketing crime, Mayor? Murder, robbery, rape, mass kidnapping, home invasions, drive by, school, mall shooting, carjacking, smash and grab, and now even arson. How about that piracy on the lake, the Vista Ferry slaughter?"

The Mayor said, "Shut your mouth. All lies you just said. You know our crime numbers get better every year. None of that's true."

Aslan heard this all. "Who would vote for this person and for what reason?"

Reuben smiled broadly. "It does not matter about the vote. Politicians use voting machines made in China with programs invented by Venezuelans, and homemade mail in ballots people can print themselves. Then drop them off in drop boxes around the city. Even dead people vote for her. It's all corrupt."

Tarmara said, "What, in the USA?"

Reuben said, "Of course. It's all in the name of anti-voter suppression, meaning let anyone vote, even more than once. They just made a new rule that illegal aliens can vote too, in City elections."

Yasmine said, "You mean we can vote too?"

"Yes, you too. You can run for office and vote," laughing out loud again.

Ramin said, "With respect, this is not funny. This is the end of democracy. Even in Kabul, under international observation, we have free and fair election."

"Well, you did not have Commonwealth voting machines, internet hackers, and fake ballots. We do. The Democrats believe it gives the minorities a bigger voice."

By now Reuben could not hold himself together, cracking up on just how stupid it all sounded, yet true.

"So, he will, I mean, she will win?"

"Yes, by more votes than there are voters, with help of the

media. No one cares. It is all corrupt. Today, in the United States, if money can fix a problem, it's not a problem, and money fixes it all."

Aslan said, "Oh my God, I am so shocked and sad for this great nation."

"Great nation, maybe," said Reuben, "Just keep your head down and nose clean and you will be fine. Don't expect honesty or fairness from our Mayor. And please don't quote me. Forget I told you."

"OK, but one question, please. Is this just Chicago or every place here?"

"Aslan, that is your name, correct? It is in most places. Most big States and Cities run by Democrats. Frankly, that is what drove poor Trump crazy. They stole the national election by corrupting six big cities. All a joke. Don't repeat what I said, they will fire me and punch my face."

'No one punches me in the face," said Ramin.

"OK, enough for one day, said Tamara. Come Ramin, come everyone, Reuben's fine food awaits us."

The breakfast tasted better than ever, fried eggs in olive oil, potatoes, no meat, toast and tea for everyone. The same time they were digesting the food, they were digesting what they had learned. Reuben had changed the TV channel. No more Mayor, at least not for now. No one approved of anything they heard.

After breakfast, the women packed some snacks and drinks for the visit to the park. This being the first day out for the women and children, they hoped it would be a fun time with the weather perfect.

"Bring your sweaters, the masks, even for the children," said Ramin. Tamara arranged everything. They were off, the children and the women, all smiles, holding hands all the way.

"Go east here, turn left, my darling wife," Ramin said to Tamara, there were giggles. She replied, "This is so beautiful. I wish for more such days, inish Allah, really I do."

Aslan and Yasmine agreed. The men said nothing, knowing these women deserved something special. A trip to Maggie Daley Park and the lake, for a picnic it seemed.

The children found the playground, merry-go-round, the slide, the swings, and could be heard repeating, "Push me Daddy, push me higher." Mona was the high flyer. Up, up, away, with screams of joy and laughter from all.

Tamara watched it all, "What a nice day it is, Aslan."

"Yes, thanks to God."

Yasmine echoed it, "Amen."

Hamid bought some ice cream from a street vendor. A nice treat.

Rocky Road, Great.

They played in the park past lunch. Aslan knew they were late.

Rashid answered for the men, "It is fine. Enjoy yourselves. You deserve it. We will buy some bread and cheese in the mini store on the way home. We are fine."

By 3:00 p.m., the children were worn out. Tamara said it was time to head home. There would be tea, white cheddar cheese, and French bread, as promised.

Back in the rooms, the children were knocked out and fast asleep. The past few days were a whirlwind for them, they needed to rest.

By 7:00 p.m., Ramin asked, "Hungry anyone or are we OK?"

Kids will be kids. They were ready for a meal.

Ramin said, "OK, a short prayer, a small dinner, and to sleep early. You need the rest."

The restaurant was full. It happened to be steak night. The food excelled. Nothing like the aroma of steak to wake up the appetite.

Bathing was fast and sleep came early. This turned out to be the first night in many that everyone enjoyed a deep and restful sleep, Thanks to God.

Tomorrow, the Mosque, to meet Moslem brothers and sisters.

Chapter 7

Next morning, prayers and breakfast were rushed. Everyone made ready for the visit to the Mosque.

"Yasmine, and the children, please remain here while we all go. So sorry, I know, again, but it is best." Yasmine answered Hamid, "I understand, it is fine. Please learn as much as you can for us all. Go with God and be safe."

"Rashid, you have the maps. We have our bus passes," said Ramin. All was in order and the adventure was on.

First order of business was what bus to take. They were going south for what appeared to be a long way. "Number 86, we got it." After some confusion boarding, it proved Rashid was right. No transfer required and they were on the way.

The driver was kind and asked everyone to sit at the front of the bus. He would tell them when to get off. The bus stopped and started almost every block, a local not express.

"This is truly an adventure," said Tamara.

Ramin gestured, "Look, so many people, men and women, all in a hurry and not many smiles."

After nearly an hour, the driver waived his hand and pointed at the Mosque. It was beautiful.

"Catch Bus 94 back, OK."

"Thank you, sir," as the group, led by Ramin, exited the Bus, heading across the street to the Mosque.

The door of the Mosque was open. The women moved to the right. Men went straight in to the center. Several members of the congregation sat on the lushly carpeted floor.

Imam Akeem sat directly ahead.

The Imam spoke, "A salaam amalecum." The group returning the greeting in unison, "A salaam amalecum and malecum salaam."

The Imam took the floor. "We have but one hour, as we greet other Brothers and Sisters all day. I am Imam Akeem. I invite you to attend our Mosque. Every day, we are here for you. Familiarize yourself with our city as much as you can these next days. When you are ready to relocate to your new homes, we will send trucks for you and we will move you."

Ramin spoke next, "Thank you all very much. We are most happy to meet you and wish to be members of this fine Mosque. This is my family and friends," and he introduced one and all.

The Imam went on, "I cannot introduce you to everyone assembled, but all of us now know you. Khalil, Noor, raise your hands, please. See them, they own the grocery store near here which is close to your new home, yes."

"Please come to our store. My wife, Noor, and I are there most days and we do stock many of our foods from home. We too are from Kabul." Noor waived at the ladies and everyone smiled.

The Imam Akeem went on, "The Mosque is open for daily prayers. You are all welcome. There is a women's club. Weekly service is held Friday at 6:30 p.m. Please come as often as possible. We welcome you."

Young Abdul and Fatima were introduced as assistants to the Imam, they offered their help.

"Faisil, do tell our new immigrants more about their new city."

"Yes, welcome. I am Faisil, from Karachi. I have been here for 12 years. Here is my contact information. I do international business. If you need anything from back home, do tell me."

"Thank you."

"You heard the Imam, and you see Khalil and Noor. Please also know Akbar and Sara. They own the Afghan / Pakistani restaurant, the Crescent, on the corner."

"Yes," called out Akbar from where he was sitting near the Imam, "Please all come. Your first meal, for all, is my gift to you in thanks to Allah, for your safe arrival."

Before anyone could reply, Faisil went on, "As for the city, you must be aware. Try to stay in groups in public. Never go out at night, certainly not alone. Do not wear your gold or jewelry outside. Do not talk to strangers. Keep your doors locked when at home – there is crime. There are many victims. It can be very violent. You must be safe."

Rashid asked, "You mean crime like robbery?"

"Yes, robbery, assault, so sorry to say, rape, even murder. There are many gangs. They fight each other over the drug trade, shooting each other. Often bystanders too. Safety is your number one concern, even for children. You will learn more, especially here at the Mosque. This Mosque is secure, the door is unlocked. I assure you, it is secure from threat."

"It cannot be worse than Kandahar, can it?" asked Ramin, starting a conversation.

"It is far, far worse than any city back home and the crime goes unpunished. This is the problem."

"Why so?"

"There is corruption. We all understand this."

"Yes," said Ramin, listening closely.

"Drug money corrupts many officials, like the Mayor."

"We heard a little about her too already."

"And, gang warfare, there are thousands of different gang members. The mafia too and all types of people. They fight for territory. This explains all the changing graffiti on the walls everywhere. There are drug dealers, drug users, and sexual perverts of all sorts."

"Crime of opportunity, even against women and children. There is robbery, mugging, burglary, home invasion, and thieves will rob your home, if you are home or not."

"New smash and grabs too. Very common and no punishment. Like to make up for past people oppression from a hundred years ago. All about social justice and being above the law."

"Above the law," answered Ramin, "I thought the law was for everyone."

"Not now. There is no criminal justice, only social justice. Many things are now justified. Politicians say it is OK, and even do not prosecute saying it is all insured, so it is not crime."

"Not a crime because paid for by insurance companies?"

"That is about it. People rob stores every day, security does nothing, even armed security does nothing."

"I am to be a Chicago Security. You mean I do nothing about crime I see?"

"You watch and report, do nothing. If you do act, you would be put in trouble. Police won't come. If they do come, they won't arrest. If they do arrest, the District Attorney will not prosecute. If they do prosecute, even with a conviction, there is no punishment."

"At least they are arrested and off the street, no?"

"No, there is no longer any prejudgment or even post-conviction incarceration – all are free and back on the street, almost at once. Most crime is committed by criminals awaiting a trial for other crimes. They have no fear, you can do nothing."

"What if I do something?"

"You will be fired from your job. If a policeman does his job, he is put into trouble. If he hurts someone, even someone doing injury to others, the policeman can be liable for any harm. This is all about supposed social justice for past oppression. Victims suffering does not matter."

"Insurance cannot replace a human life."

"Don't even think of revenge, you can be arrested and punished."

Ramin seemed aggrieved, "This is not fair. This is not equal treatment."

"True, Ramin, this is chaos worse than in Kabul. This is not freedom. It is oppression of the innocent."

Aslan had to ask, "Faisil, do you mean in Chicago or every place in the USA?"

"Aslan, it is in every place, all of the big cities. Some worse than others. Here in Chicago, New York, St. Louis, San Francisco, Seattle, Los Angeles. Chicago is the very worst."

"Disgraceful," said Aslan, "This is not God's way."

"We need guns, then, for self-protection, right?" asked Ramin.

"Well, you may need them, but there is strict gun control, it is the bad guys that have most of the guns."

Ramin smiled, "Well, we have our pocket knives."

Imam Akeem waived his hand, "Unless there is a God-driven

event, to bring God back into city life, we are powerless to change anything."

Rashid, ever the optimist said, "The elections can change things, like back home."

Faisil said, "The elections are fake. The government and media cover it all up."

Rashid responded at once, "This is not a free country then. It is a prison camp for victim suffering."

The Imam cut in, "My son, you do not want to speak out. They will cancel you and destroy you to silence you. They do not tolerate dissent. It is best to know and not say."

"Enough of this, please," said Imam Akeem. "We have no more time. We are here to help you live safely, God willing, to be a part of our Moslem community. There are over 40 Mosques in Chicago. All of us do what we can to live God's good life of freedom, faith and mutual support. We are here to help you too."

Other men sitting around the room, said the same, "We are your neighbors. We all live nearby. Take our names. We are all brothers and sisters."

Ramin could see Afghanis in the room, Pakistanis, people from Chechnya, some from Uzbekistan and Turkistan. All devout Moslems. It would be OK.

One last thing, Rashid asked, "What about this Black Moslem group here. Is it good?"

The Imam Akeem answered, holding his hand up to slow down Faisil, "They are brothers in Islam. They have their own Mosque, newspapers and teach the teachings of the Prophet. The praise be unto him, in their own way, with their own leader, they work hard. They keep their family and do not do crime – they too have to deal with the chaos on the street. They like us. Godly people. We respect them as brothers in faith."

"Go now, find your way home by Bus. We will come for you when you ask. There are some gifts on the table for you. Baklava too, please take. Be safe and we shall see you all soon."

The group got up, said their goodbyes, took the gifts, and left for the LaQuinta. "Thank you, we shall see you all soon, inish Allah," said Rashid.

Ramin walked over to the Imam to thank him and over to Faisil, "Thank you, my dear brothers, I hope to see you again."

"You shall, inish Allah, every week. Call me and I will visit. We are friends. We know your background. I was a Captain too, in the Pakistani forces, on the border. We are one."

With that, the group left. Khalil went with them, to go back to his store.

Just outside the Mosque, sure enough, a big yellow car sped by. People yelled, "Go back to where you came from, towel heads."

Aslan asked, "What is a towel head? We do not wear towels on our head."

Ramin knew what it meant. He knew it was threatening. He did not like it. If he held his old XM177 Commando, the yelling would have stopped. His years of training kicked in. He would not forget this car, those people.

Chapter 8

The trip back to the hotel was easier, seemed faster, Bus 94 was on time, and the strangers on board looked more familiar this time. Soon, they were in the Lobby, it was lunch, and they joined Yasmine and the children, over southern fried chicken.

"Daddy, try the wings with the red sauce, it is like back home, try it Daddy," said Jamil to Ramin, and he was right, the food was delicious, thanks to God.

Lunch was calming at the LaQuinta, safe and secure, but Ramin, Rashid, even Hamid, all had a new foreboding feeling about their new home.

Magi and Mona were done with their food, Mona was waiving to everyone, "Mommy, please, I know you are tired, but can we just walk over to the lake to see the water, feel the sun, please?"

Mona was the oldest child, two years older than Magi, she had done much to take care of the other children, for days now. Aslan answered, checking with Rashid for the green light, "Yes, we shall all go out for a short while for some fresh air."

Talk about a happy family, Yasmine walked with the women and children, all holding hands, listening to the whole story about the visit to the Mosque.

"Ok, I understand all, let us enjoy the moment with the children, we talk more later, God willing we are safe, in God's hands, children, there is the park and the big, blue lake."

The lake glistened, the children's voices could be heard loud and clear – it was a fun for all. The adults kept a better watch on each other, the children, and their new environment.

"We fear nothing," said Ramin, to anyone within earshot, "but we must be aware of any situation, like back home, just worse."

"It will soon be dark, everyone ready to head back to the hotel?" asked Rashid. No objection, the group of happy travelers headed home.

"Tomorrow we shall all go to visit this Mrs. Jinx," said Rashid, "to see our new homes."

Chapter 9

The LaQuinta had become a safe haven for the children. They all enjoyed watching cartoons on TV and laughed together. It filled Ramin's room with happy sounds. The adults sat together reviewing events, reading the housing and employment papers in preparation to see Mrs. Jinx the next day.

"We will go as a group to learn all about our future in this new city," said Rashid. Aslan cut in, "We will see everything, Tamara. We should bring pen and paper to write down the things we will need to make our new homes complete, yes?"

Tamara answered, "Good idea. We will go after breakfast."

Ramin, "Yes, good idea. God willing, we will know more tomorrow."

Rashid pulled out the map book, "Let me show you some places on the map, Ramin."

"Sure, shoot."

"Here is the lake and downtown LaQuinta. You can see the north side down to the South Shore."

"Yes, I see."

"Here is China Town. The red dots are Mosques. There are many. This red star is our new Mosque and the green dot is our new home address. Do you see?"

"Yes, yes, very good."

"There are so many parks, open spaces, big roads, and

colleges. So many."

"Around our new digs you can see the districts like Englewood, Garfield, Washington, Park, Lawndale and Grande Crossing. Here is Riverdale," Rashid pointed each location out on the map, "Chatham, South Shore – remember, Avalon Park, Deering, Pullman, Fuller, Auburn and Chicago Dawn. So many."

"And, as you can see this is shopping that is close to us?"

"Very good, Rashid."

"There is this problem. Faisil is correct."

"What problem?"

"The Crime. It is everyplace. It says here 85% of the people in our area feel it is unsafe to walk the streets. The government crime data says people have a one in ten chance of becoming a victim of violent crime."

"Hard to believe," said Ramin, "that people accept to live under such a situation which is far, far worse than anything back home."

"It has gone on for decades and gets worse every year."

"What about the police department, do they not fight crime in the streets?"

"The police mostly are honest. Some are not. But none of them fight crime today," as Faisil said. "Their salary, pension, retirement is all in danger. There is the movement, in the Democratic cities around the nation, to defund the police. Meaning taking away their budget money, resources and equipment."

"Defund the police, then what?"

"Mayor Heavyhand and most Democrat elected leaders agree

to cut down the police and let the people of the community police themselves. Meaning the gangs with guns will rule the streets. They would be community collective in control. This fits with the plan for no bail or jail. Small crimes not being crimes at all including many violent crimes as well. And no punishment."

"This is happening now?"

"Yes. That is why, if you call the police they don't come until the next day, if at all. A joke, really."

"How do people live like this? I have no words, Rashid, to express myself. People do not live like this anyplace in the world. Do the Americans not realize this?"

"They do, but they cannot do anything about it. Just hope nothing bad happens to them."

"This means the women and the children are not safe. What are we to do? They cannot defend themselves. I am now worried, Rashid. Worried about you too!"

Ramin got up. "OK, for now, we must make this our home. As we learn more the brothers and sisters at the Mosque will help. We must go to services and participate as much as possible."

Yasmine and Aslan shook their heads in agreement. Tamara added, "Yes, God willing. We shall join the Men's Club, the Women's Club, and for sure enroll the children in the school of the Mosque. It has classes every weekend."

With that, it was time to pray and have dinner. Ramin waived the children over for prayer.

Getting off the elevator, the air was heavy with the sweet aroma of curry. "Great, Daddy," Jamil burst out, "I love curry."

"Me too, son. Let us all go and enjoy. If you see any staff, you must tell them thank you."

There was plenty of rice too. "I love the rice, Daddy." Everyone was happy for the rice and the curry.

Thanks to God for everything. Reuben had done a great job.

Chapter 10

The next morning was like moving his platoon back home, Ramin thought, now with nine members strong on their way to the bus stop. Going south to their new homes they were excited and unsure, not knowing what they would find. When asked, the driver said, "Stay on the bus. It will take about one hour. I will signal you. Sit down and relax."

All the way there, everyone peered out the windows. This was a big adventure, seeing so many new places and fast cars going back and forth. There are so many new people too. The excitement made Mona hungry and nervous. "Mommy, did you bring some bread to snack on?"

"Oh my, hungry already? Yes, here is a nice, fresh piece of bread with butter for you."

"Thank you. Hmm, this is really good."

Neither Rashid or Ramin saw any street violence on the way. All seemed calm, yet wondering what was the reality out there. They would soon find out.

"There it is, the Hampton Court Apartments. See the big HCA. That is our new place," said Rashid. "Let's get off here." They all crossed the street. They were standing in front of their new home.

"Mr. Everett said we would be on the second floor. Find Mrs. Jinx in Apartment 1. Who is to knock and introduce us all?"

"Of course, Rashid, be my guest," said his wife, Aslan. Ramin pointed to the door making a knocking motion. He knocked three times.

Mrs. Jinx's door had 3 locks and a peep hole. "Who is it? Is it Ramin? You came?"

"Yes, it is Ramin and my family. Thank you."

"I see you. Very good, let me open the door. You don't see anyone else around you, do you?"

"No."

With that the door opened and Mrs. Jinx said, "Please come straight in. I don't like to keep my door open."

"You must be Ramin and Rashid, right? Let's see, you're Hamid, this is your wife Yasmine, and the children. I don't know their names."

Hamid answered, "That is Jamil, son of Ramin and Tamara. Over there, Magi and Mona, daughters of Rashid and Aslan to your left. Thank you. So nice to meet you, Mrs. Jinx."

Mrs. Jinx asked, "Do you have children, Hamid?" This prompted Yasmine to tell her, "We did, but she was taken from us in an attack some years ago. We do not know of her now."

"I am so sorry to hear that. Well, there is still time for more," a smiling Mrs. Jinx offered.

"Well, down to business. Here are your keys. All apartments are on the 2nd floor, adjoining each other. Each apartment has been refurbished and all have in home laundry."

"Oh, thank you," Yasmine replied, before she could continue.

"The good news is your rent and utilities are paid for one year and trash and recycle services as well. No pets. No overnight guests unless you notify me. And this is important. Always keep your door locked and be sure to close your curtains at night."

Ramin asked if she lived alone. Mrs. Jinx said, "Yes, my dear husband died just over a year ago, so I am alone."

"Not to worry, Mrs. Jinx, he is in a better place. You are always welcome to visit us. Come for dinner too, once we are settled. You will like the food."

Everyone echoed Ramin's invitation.

"Thank you. Shall we go and see your new homes? How exciting?"

"Yes, Mrs. Jinx, let us go," answered Ramin. Off they all went. Mrs. Jinx explained the surrounding.

"We have 36 units here and parking for one car per unit when once you get cars. The lights all around the property are on all night for security. At 5:00 p.m. the front and back gates, like the one you just came through, are locked. Your keys will unlock it."

"Please do not lose your key, no matter what, except the post box key. You may not need it. They may not deliver mail anymore. There have been too many mailmen robbed and killed trying to deliver. Don't expect any mail."

"So, here we are. Go in and inspect your new homes. If there is anything I need to do, let me know. I will wait here."

The apartments were indeed clean, nice, with new appliances, carpet, window coverings and a good size too.

Ramin noticed the women making notes, hearing Aslan say, "Yes, write it down. We need mops, brooms, cleaning items, soap, shampoo, sponges, towels and paper napkins. There are beautiful plates, pots and pans, and cutlery already here. There are trash cans and trash bags as well."

"Don't forget food. A hungry man is an angry man. The middle eastern and far eastern store is right across the street. Khalil told me he had already met you. That's wonderful. He and his wife Noor are so nice."

Aslan heard her, "Yes, we did. We also met Akbar and Sara, at the Crescent restaurant. Is it close by?"

"Yes, just down the block. Oh my, what delicious food. I suppose you cook just as well."

"You have been there?"

"Yes, Aslan, many times. My husband was enchanted by the food and the people are so kind. You will love it too."

"Yes, inish Allah. Yes, let us all go one day."

"If you have time I will drive you down to the store to buy the things on your list. That way you won't have to carry it all. How about having Yasmine and Aslan go with me and one of the men. All the others can wait in my apartment."

"Yes, that is good. I will accompany you," said Ramin, "Rashid, Hamid and Tamara, please stay here with the children. We will be quick. If you think of anything else, call us."

Mrs. Jinx drove an old, but nice, Crown Vic. "It was my husband's favorite car. I cannot sell it," she said. It had room for everyone and off they went.

Going into the store, it was obvious it had everything and many of the foods they liked so much. The women, in a flock, went through the store gathering the things they needed.

"Hello Ramin, everyone. Peace be unto you. Welcome to our store. So nice to see you. Hello Mrs. Jinx. Have all of you moved in yet?" Khalil asked.

Ramin stood with Khalil, "Not yet. We visit today to get a lay of the land. We will move soon. Thank you."

"Good. Noor will be happy to have new girlfriends close by."

"We are very happy to know you too and be so close my brother."

"Equally true."

They were indeed quick. In no time, Ramin paid, with a big smile toward the others. "I see you kindly found some of our favorite foods to take back to the hotel. Very good."

Yasmine heard, "Yes, dear Ramin, we got your favorite cheese too."

The massive trunk of the Crown Vic was full.

Everything was soon unloaded into the apartments. The group was saying their goodbyes inside the home of Mrs. Jinx when there was a knock on the door. She answered.

"Hello Diana. Perfect timing. Come and meet your new neighbors. This is Diana. She lives in Apartment 5 just down from your new homes. She works swing shift at the Chicago Police Department. Nice uniform, right?"

This started a long and happy session of greetings and Diana welcomed them all to the complex. "So nice to have new neighbors. I cannot wait for you to come and visit me. I make a great cheesecake."

"Yes, thank you, you met my son, Jamil, and Aslan's children, Mona and Magi. I hope you like children. We do not want to be noisy or disturb you, right children?"

"I love children, I have none."

What Diana did not say was during her rookie days with the CPD, working her way up to making Captain in the Intel Division, she was shot in the stomach and could not conceive. She loved children. Never able to have one, like so many victims of crime, their suffering goes unrecognized.

Ramin, a warrior himself, was severely wounded twice in the war, somehow he had an inkling. He could tell but did not say so.

"Once we move in, you, along with Mrs. Jinx, shall be our guest for dinner." Tamara asked Jamil as well, "Right, Jamil?"

"Yes, Mommy. Yes, for sure. Can we have lamb?"

"We must ask our guests if they like lamb."

"OK. Miss, do you like Lamb?"

Diana answered for both, "Yes, we do, a lot," with a warm smile while gently touching Jamil's head. "You have such nice hair, Jamil." With that compliment, the little boy blushed red, causing his mother to hug him close. "He is shy."

"Inish Allah. Then, it shall be," said Rashid, "I know our dear women and children need to make new friends in our new country, so thank you."

"We all need friends. That is so true," said Diana.

He went on, "Speaking for all of us," motioning to his brother and the others. "Everyone we have met in the USA, Mr. Everett, the people at the hotel, Reuben, Maria, Lakeysa, the clerks at the stores, the bus drivers, now Mrs. Jinx, the brothers and sisters at the Mosque, now you – everyone has been so kind. Like all our old American friends, the ones back home, may God bless and keep you all."

"Thanks, Rashid. Americans are gracious and sharing people. Welcome to our country. There are bad people here too that work the system and disregard the law. They don't care about anyone but themselves. There are even killers walking free, so do be careful."

"We have heard this. We had hoped we left that sort of thing behind. By the grace of God, we escaped Kabul, yet there are problems."

"Escaped by the grace of God," Diana replied, "We watched in horror Online what the Brandon government and the Democrat politicians did and how they did it in Kabul, your country. It is a sad disgrace and humiliation that did not have to happen."

Hearing this, Ramin could not keep silent. "God bless you. You are an intelligent and fine person. We respect you for what you just said. We try to forget it, leaving 9,000 Americans behind. Yet we are here. This is not our fault. It should have been done differently, successfully, not a failure like it was. We have no words to tell you."

"I must go run some errands before work, Mrs. Jinx. I came by to return your bottle opener. I bought one. Thank you. Oh, here is my card. Call me anytime."

Ramin thought it was nice his neighbor carried a Glock.

Chapter 11

Everyone had a mask, but no one remembered to put it on indoors. That was OK. The group said their goodbyes and were soon on the bus back to the LaQuinta.

The bus was full and made many stops. People were in a hurry to get home. No one bothered anyone. There was little talk. Let's just get home. It is time for dinner and the children are hungry. It was a nice day, filled with nice places and fine American people.

"It is Fish and Chips," Reuben said to Rashid, who was staring at it wondering what exactly it was, "You will like it. It is fried cod and chips. Use vinegar on the fish and mayo on the chips. Hmmm good."

That is what they all ate, along with some greens. Rashid later told Reuben, "Right on. That was tasty. I have never had anything like it before. Thank you."

Later it was time for a prayer, baths and sleep. "We will plan for tomorrow, tomorrow," Aslan said to the group. "We are all so tired yet relieved at what we learned today."

Lights out.

The next morning, the usual meeting in Ramin's room for early prayers and a surprise. Tamara announced with a big smile, "OK, everyone, we have an Afghan breakfast in the room."

"I have coffee, tea and milk for all of us. From the store I have bread, cheese, olives, zata and vinegar eggs. Let's dig in."

"This is like home, Mommy," said Magi. Everyone enjoyed the change. It was delicious.

Then, Rashid's cell phone rang. It was Faisil. "I come to pick you up in my truck. I can bring six people and drive around the city to see your new homes, places of work, and the children's school. Bring your papers and we will explore, OK?"

Rashid told the others and replied, "Thank you very much. We will see you in the lobby at 8:00 a.m. We are ready now. Thank you, brother."

Someone had to stay with the children. It was Yasmine again. The other five went down to await Faisil's arrival. "We will bring you many pictures, OK?" said Tamara, hugging everyone on the way out the door.

"OK," Yasmine said. "But I must warn you. There may not be any Afghan food here by the time you get back."

Beep, Beep, it was Faisil on the horn. "You have your papers and map, yes?" he asked Ramin.

"Yes, everything. Let us first show you our new apartments, please."

Off they went through the busy morning Chicago streets, going south and exploring.

"This is so nice, brother. An F150. Please enjoy it in good health and prosperity."

"Right, Ramin, F150 and King Cab. One day you will have one too. It is the best truck in the States – 40,000,000 sold."

Ramin knew this F150 was expensive. That made him a little curious. At the same time, his sharp nose picked up the light scent of Hoppes. Knowing that a newly cleaned piece was close by gave him a sly smile. Very good, he thought to himself.

Tamara heard the music go on. "Faisil, what nice music in your truck. Such a nice truck to ride in. Thank you."

"Yes, music direct from Lahore. I am glad you like it. This is Abida. What a voice. I also have Ghazel."

"We love both of them," she replied. "We do listen to Pakistani music and we watch TV, but we do not dance."

Aslan cut in, "Yes, we also like Farhad Darya and Mahwash, Afghanis."

"I don't have them. I will check." The truck rolled along and seemed to rock to the music.

"I'm now driving by the children's school. I think they go to Elgin School?"

"Yes, let us please stop. Look, you can see the park and the school, right, Tamara?" asked Aslan.

"Yes, Aslan, let's stop and look for a moment. I want to see it."

Not long after, everyone was standing in Elgin Park, across from the school, admiring how modern the school was. The school has grades K to 6th. All three children can go to the same school.

"Thank you, Faisil and Ramin, my dear husband. What do you think? Perfect, yes?"

"Yes, it is very beautiful and new. It is only a two-block walk from our apartment over there," pointing west. "You see it, Faisil?" Everyone turned to see Faisil nodding his head in agreement.

It was still very early, so the park was nearly empty except for some homeless people sleeping under nearby trees. Faisil let them know, "Those people over there, and more you don't see in the trees, they are homeless. Usually using drugs, some are violent criminals. Be sure, ladies, to stay far away from them. Tell the children too."

There were too many of these types of people in the park for Ramin's liking. He stared hard at them. "There are so many in this one park. This is not really a safe place, Aslan and Tamara. You must be very careful about this park."

Faisil waived his hand, "OK, let's go to your apartments. I want to see where you will live. Then we will go one by one to your future work places. We will go now."

Aslan, at the same time, could be heard talking to the children. "No children, not today. We have no time to play in the park. Next time, but we must stay away from strangers. Remember that."

It was very simple. Two blocks down Elgin Street from Elgin School, and they were in the parking lot of the Hampton Court Apartments. The big HCA sign read "HCA. Private Property. Violators Will Be Towed Away."

Faisil thought it looked very nice. "We don't have to go inside, unless you must. It is a good start for you. I shall come again, God willing. We should go on. What should be next, Rashid?"

"The closest is Chicago Security, for Ramin, on Ashland. Then we can go to Mercy EMT on South California, for Hamid. I will come last. The Tribunal newspaper, it is the furthest away on Grand. My papers say I will later work out of a satellite office, closer in."

"OK, jump in and let's go. I will drive on the streets and your bus will follow, so pay attention."

Anyway they went, Faisil, along with Ramin, Rashid, Hamid, Aslan and Tamara, with the music on and the windows down, the air was so fresh, and Aslan and Tamara had pieces of Turkish Delight snacks.

"This is so good," said Aslan, for all to hear. Faisil looked into the rear view mirror, where he could see Aslan smiling, "I like Turkish Delight too."

With a laugh, the box of Turkish Delight was passed to the front, for all to share.

"You have a sweet tooth, Faisil?" asked Aslan.

"Yes, I confess, it is true."

"We have an invitation from our lovely neighbor, Diana, to visit for what she calls cheesecake dessert. When we go, you must come too. God willing, OK?"

"Deal. Text me when and I will be there, jolly on the spot."

Aslan could see his smile in the mirror and she hoped this would come to pass. Faisil was single. She thought, one never knows.

"There is Chicago Security, a big place and close to your apartment, Ramin."

"Yes, I see. That was fast. OK, so I will come here next week, maybe Wednesday. I will call them. Can you go around the block? I would like to see more."

"Sure, how's that?"

"Fine, thank you. Where to now, Rashid?"

"Mercy EMT on South California."

"Good, that is close too. Maybe two minutes by car. We are on the way."

Hamid heard Faisil, but he did not answer. He was busy looking out the window, seeing so many boarded up buildings, bars, liquor stores, and dance clubs. It seemed a funny place for an EMT.

"There it is on the right. Nice office."

"Yes, Faisil, very nice. They said I would be Intern Training and working in the office. So that is where I will come to work. It looks very qualified."

"I will go around the back. Oh, look, there is your bus stop too. OK?"

"Thank you, again. So now to the Tribunal for Rashid, right?"

Rashid answered in the affirmative. Now Ghazel was singing to the party and it was soothing to the nerves to hear.

Faisil, talking to Rashid, "This will be a longer bus ride for you and a 15 minute drive for us. If you get to work at a satellite office, closer by, that would be excellent."

"Yes, I will come to the main office next week and I think they will assignment me to a closer office."

"You saw what you need to see?"

"Yes, thank you. Let's bring Faisil to lunch now, OK?"

"Thank you. I am a little hungry. I will join you."

"I will call Yasmine to join us with the children, downstairs, in 15 minutes, right?"

"Yes," replied Aslan. "But we should go to our rooms to clean up a little and say a short prayer, and fetch Yasmine, if agreeable, my dear husband."

"That is what we shall do, with your approval, Faisil. You can come up too, please."

"Deal." Faisil was accustomed to saying 'deal,' maybe because he was a businessman. He parked and everyone was surprised parking cost $6.00 an hour. "No worry he said, I got it. Let's eat. I had a really small breakfast."

Ramin could see Faisil had no problem about money. He carried a nice size wad of bills.

Back upstairs, Yasmine had all the questions and they gave her all the answers while they cleaned up for lunch. They said a short mid-day prayer before going downstairs.

The menu sign in the lobby said, 'Irish Lamb Stew.' That sounded appealing to everyone on board.

"Ready, let us go," said Yasmin. And in they went. Faisil and Ramin stopped at the door to watch a TV news report.

"Fox 32 can now report that 32 people were shot in Chicago yesterday. The first fatal shooting occurred at 6:30 p.m. in the 9000 block of South Harper Avenue when a young male was shot in the head while sitting inside a vehicle. The second fatal shooting took place at 8:40 p.m. when a 27 year old man was shot and killed while walking on the sidewalk in the 8100 block of South Ingleside Avenue. A full listing of shootings can be found on our website. This brings the total number of shootings for the year-to-date to 1,677, adding to the recently released total of 11,869 shootings from last year, as the violent crime wave goes into its 11th year, nonstop."

"Faisil, this is a war zone. It is worse than back home. Even at the height of the fighting?"

"True. Not just in Chicago, in most big cities in the USA. You will see. Democrat Party politics defund the police, no law enforcement, releases after repeated arrests without bond and juveniles never punished for anything. There is no incarceration even if a criminal is found guilty. There is early release for killers. It makes crime legal so the streets are dangerous."

"Why do people accept this, Faisil?"

"People don't, but they can do nothing about it. The elections are fixed by the Democrats and politicians and the judges are Democrats too. They believe social justice is more important than public safety. It is to bad for victims. Chaos is OK. Let's eat."

"OK, but you are saying the country is so big no one cares?"

"People care. If anyone speaks out, they are attacked by the Democrats, the media it controls as racist. Everything and everyone is a racist, especially if people are for peace and public safety. No one wants to be attacked on social media or in the news."

"I was told, when we came over, never say anything. Not even at work. I understand better now. I had more freedom to talk back home than here. What a bad joke."

"The food is good. Come on, let's get it while its hot and fresh." With that, Faisil and Ramin joined the rest of the group.

This time it was Mona. She called out, "Daddy, this stew is sort of like what grandmother makes. It is delicious. Thank you." Magi and Jamil both agreed.

"Thanks to God and the American taxpayer," answered Faisil before Ramin could say a word. He was worrying, wondering how to keep his family safe in this strange world.

So many hard working, good people. So much evil promoted by a few. So many helpless victims.

Lunch was soon done. Faisil bid his farewell. "Call me when you move. I will bring my truck to help," as he quickly disappeared.

It had been a busy day and a big lunch. Tamara said it out loud, "Time for a nap."

No argument.

Chapter 12

As the children napped, the adults scoured the news on their cell phones and watched some local TV. By the time afternoon prayers and dinner rolled around, they all had a good idea of what life was like in urban America.

Using Telegram, the best message service Online, by 6:00 p.m., each of them had called home at least once to chat with relatives. Calling was not uncommon for them, but this day everyone called a loved one.

The news from home was not good. Food was scarce, reprisals were commonplace against perceived enemies of the Taliban, and thousands of Americans and supporters were still trying to escape. Ramin was heard to discuss various land routes to Pakistan, Uzbekistan and Turkmenistan. All of this was expected to go on for weeks, if not months.

Aslan was on her cell, "We are all fine. Thanks to God and the gracious Americans, we are all safe. We have been provided all we need. Soon we will relocate to our new apartments. Yes, we will keep you updated."

"That is great news, Aslan." This was heard by everyone as she was on the speaker phone. "God willing all works out. Keep us informed. Have faith in God. Allah Akbar."

Later that evening, before bedtime, Rashid's telephone rang. "Hello Faisil, so soon to hear from you. What's up? Say that again, please. OK, thank you."

Rashid addressed the family. "That was Faisil. He is sending his friend, Aziz, over tomorrow to fetch us at 7:30 a.m. to take us to the Social Security Office, do our tax, and banking. He is the expert."

Hearing this, Hamid said, "We have to pay tax? Wow!"

"No, it's something else. We must bring all of our papers for everyone and do what Aziz says. Plan to spend the entire day."

"Ladies and children, you will stay here all day tomorrow to relax and study English. We will see you at the end of the day."

Chapter 13

Right on time, 7:30 a.m. sharp, a big black Chrysler 300 was waiting for the men outside with the windows down. "Rashid. Ramin. It is me, Aziz. Please join me."

In a jiff, and after several greetings back and forth, and introductions, the car whisked off.

"I am taking you to the Social Security Office to get Social Security Cards for you. The card has a number on it and you should memorize it. You need it for everything including banking, school, work and tax. It is for your pension and benefits in the future and medical care when you are older."

It was Ramin's turn, he was riding shotgun. "Thank you, Aziz. We are indebted to you for your help. We hope everyone to be great friends and one day return your kindness."

"You are welcome. I will help all of you. We have many stops today; Social Security, my Accountants, Edgar and Wilbur Castello, and the Chase Bank. You shall see."

Social Security was a large and busy office. People wore masks but it was like business as usual. The entire group was called into an office and the process went pretty fast.

"I am Officer Olivia Gonzales, please, each of you, say your names and give me all your papers. Welcome to the United States of America. See our flag in the corner of my office," pointing to it behind her. "Now this is all our flag. Please sit down."

"Let me start with you Rashid. I have all your information here. I will input and you will review it. If OK, please sign off for everyone. Agreed?"

"Yes, thank you."

In a few minutes, Rashid was signing the final document and he was given temporary proof of social security numbers for himself, his wife, and the children.

"Next up, Ramin, you know the drill. So let's go on. I see here you were a Captain. Very good and thank you for your service."

Ramin did not answer, but nodded his head and smiled.

Soon, Ramin was signing the final document, and he was given temporary proof of social security numbers for himself, his wife, and child.

"Thank you very much," Ramin said. Rashid, who somehow forgot to thank the officer, stood up and said, "Please forgive me. Thank you very much madam."

"You are welcome. OK, Hamid, let's look at your papers. Give me a few minutes, please."

"I see no children. Is that correct?"

"Yes, madam."

Officer Olivia passed the final papers over to Hamid to read and sign. Which he did. He also was given temporary proof of social security numbers for himself and his wife.

"Gentlemen, please remember your new numbers. Your permanent cards will come in the mail to your new address. Watch for your mail in about three weeks. And, Aziz, nice to see you again. It is nice of you to help so many people."

Aziz answered for the group. "No, thank you. Everyone on your feet. We have things to do and more kind people to see."

Everyone was surprised at how smooth the office visit went. Ramin was impressed. "That was amazing. Back home a visit to a government official, oh my God, would take hours and who knows how much bakshish to get anything done."

"I know. I am from Egypt. It is the same there. Thanks to God, it is better. Now, we must go and see my accountant, Wilbur Castillo. His partner, Edgar, is in Mexico, so Wilbur will do tax for all of you."

Hamid had to ask. "Why do we pay tax, so soon already?"

Aziz laughed before he replied. "You don't pay, you get paid, no matter if you are citizens or not. Even illegals qualify. No matter if you never worked or have ever paid in, even one cent of income tax, Social Security or Medicare. You still will get good money in your hands today. Not just you, anyone, especially those that do not work."

Ramin, "How can this be?"

"Well, President Brandon and the Democrats are socialist communists and this is their system. You don't need to have worked, not even to look for work. You have no obligation to look for or undertake a job. You don't have to do anything. If you claim you are poor, you will be paid."

"Of course, if you don't work, you will be poor."

"Sort of, Ramin, the poor want to stay poor. You see, look over there, the Burgers King. And there too, look, at the Sweet Tomatoes. Help Wanted. No one goes to work because people are afraid if they go to work they will have to pay tax; Social Security, Medicare. They may lose the government payment you are about to receive, today."

"You are saying people do not want to work, and they pay no tax, social security, nothing, to the government. Yet the government pays them. How can the government pay if it gets no money?"

"Exactly. For Democrats, it is fine. They just borrow more. The national debt here is over 30 trillion dollars. Maybe next year the interest on the debt will be one trillion dollars a year, so they will borrow more to pay the interest too."

Rashid knew this was all delusional. "This President Brandon, the Democrats, remember, they left for free $90,000,000,000 of military equipment back home, for the Taliban and they pay the poor to stay home and stay poor. How many poor?"

"Millions of poor and more every day. We have 80,000 alone just from your country and get this, 6,000,000 people, all poor, coming across our border from Mexico, this year alone. About 4,000,000 are caught, the rest disappear. They all get an IPEN number as illegal aliens. They cannot get a social security card but they still get the same tax refunds you will get today. This is one big reason millions come in."

Rashid had read about this, "You know that only about half the people President Brandon brought from our country should have been allowed here. The rest are really terrorists and criminals. Why do that?"

"Rashid, the Democrats are communists and they are fine with criminals and terrorists. They are really mental cases and we know, don't we, this creates a great risk to public safety here. It is insane, but it is true."

"OK, but why bring in more over the southern border? Do not the border forces stop it?"

"Good question, Rashid. The Democrats want two classes of people in the U.S.A. The rich, like the tech and international oligarchs that support them and the poor, so the Democrat Socialists can control the poor with the power money and get their vote. More and more, like in Chicago, they allow illegal aliens to vote. You will soon see the power; they get milk money, food stamps, Section 8 public housing payments, or public housing, welfare money, medical care, education and tutors, free transportation, and more, plus the tax refund. They expect the poor to do as they are told."

"Aziz, how can anyone get a tax refund when no one paid any tax?"

"Rashid, that is Democrat Party magic. They call it a tax refund as it comes from the Internal Revenue Tax Authority. But it is nothing more than a transfer payment, a gift, and a big one, as you will see."

Ramin thought this was nonsense.

"Aziz, I believe every word. This system seems doomed. It cannot be sustained. It will destroy the nation, no doubt about it."

"Ramin, already the top 1% of Americans have more wealth than the entire middle class. The middle sinks like a rock, under the weight of tax, massive inflation, the cost of living, college, the silent killers, like medical care and insurance. The middle class will soon all be poor, which is what the Democrats want, rich and dependent poor people. They promise legal drugs, pornography, legalized pedophilia, like the new lady on the Supreme Court does. People already cannot afford the $9.00 quarter pounder hamburger at MacDonalds, laughing out loud. Not including fries or drink. What a joke."

Ramin asked the 64,000 Dollar Question. "Why should we work?"

"Well, you have jobs already. Go and see how it is. If you don't like it, don't work. You could get the highest benefits if you never work. It is crazy."

"Wow," was heard all around the interior of the car.

"Here we are now. Get my Accountant's card and stay in touch with him. You will need him. I make the introductions. Let's go in."

The office of Edgar and Wilbur Castillo was not big but it was packed with what people call tax payers. Few, if any of them, pay tax. They collect tax credits and refunds.

Wilbur saw Aziz. "Aziz, mi amigo, venga aqui, are these my new clients?"

"Yes, hello Wilbur," gently waving to him as he was engaged with another tax payer. "Yes, this is Ramin, Rashid and Hamid, three new families, all with Social Security cards."

"Wonderful, everyone come sit at the desk. Good to see new clients. Welcome. Who goes first?"

Aziz answered for the group. "Please my amigo, start with Rashid, then Ramin, and Hamid. They are all new in the U.S, have never worked nor paid any tax or withholding, and they need the maximum Tax Refund."

"OK, great. These are easy and fast tax reports and all the same with lots of zeros and a big check for each. Great country, the USA. It prints money and gives it away."

In no time at all, amazing to see for the new refugees, three stacks of tax papers were placed before them for review and signature. They could see their names and addresses, family relations, and numbers showing refunds.

"If everything is correct, please sign, in your own language or English using whatever your signature is, as you used at the Social Security Office and try to maintain that signature from now on."

Everyone signed in short order and handed the tax reports back to Wilbur.

"OK, I will file all of this for you electronically and by mail to be safe. I shall give you each one copy in a file folder. Please keep your papers. There are lots of papers in the U.S., in the folders, for next year."

He went on. "Now the happy part, Rashid, Aslan, Magi, and Mona, your family will receive a tax refund of $22,000.00Federal and State. You can await it in the mail from the IRS or you can assign it to me and I will issue you a check for $20,500.00, charging you $1,500.00 in fees for my work."

"Give them a check. They will assign. Everyone will do the same," answered Aziz.

Wilbur passed over to the new taxpayers the three assignments to sign. "Same signature, please," and he took his check book out of his side drawer.

"OK, for Rashid and Aslan, $20,500.00."

"Ramin, Tamara and Jamil, your tax refund is $18,500.00, and I will give you $17,000.00, again, $1,500.00 for my services."

"Hamid and Yasmine, only $2,500.00, no children and I charge no fee."

Ramin looked at Hamid, he was somewhat disappointed. "No worry, Hamid, Rashid and I will each give you $2,000.00, so you have $6,500.00 total."

Wilbur overheard, he had to say it out loud, "Well, you are honest taxpayers, many people come in, I wonder if these different adults show up with the same children, use different names, get the IPEN numbers, claim them, over and over again, no documents, no birth certificates, no DNA, just give away the money, in the thousands. No wonder illegal aliens are crashing our borders - they get paid to do it, by you, the taxpayers, laughing out loud."

"Thank you, my brothers," and Hamid went on, "so Wilbur, we can do this once a year? Did we get the maximum?"

"Yes, there is no maximum. You see my assistant over there, Bolivia, with Mr. Senegal. That tax payer has never worked nor has his wife. They have never paid a penny in tax, Social Security, or Medicare. Nothing, and they have five children. Actually two are still in Haiti, but no one knows. LOL. And I am to write him a check for $26,000.00 right now. Watch and see with your own eyes."

"Mr. Senegal and his wife will never get a job, won't work for fear of losing the money. They are adopting two more children in Haiti now, to increase their check next year to over $32,000.00."

"Wilbur, this check in my hand," said Ramin, "I can put this in the bank? It is mine and I do not have to pay tax on it? It is tax free too?"

"Exactly, it is a Tax Refund, laughing out loud. A small part of the $6,000,000,000.00 a day the great U.S. spends that it does not have. It just adds to the national debt. No worry. It is your money."

"Thank you, Wilbur." Aziz moved towards the closed door. "We will see you again soon. We shall take our leave to go to the Bank."

Rashid just shook his head. "Brothers, I am in shock. I cannot accept what I just witnessed. To be a part of this is totally crazy. Who thinks like this on earth?"

Wilbur, looked at the refugees. "You are now expected to be Democrats, to do what you are told, to vote for President Brandon. That is the point. The Democrats expect all the poor, the blacks in particular, the Latinos, the new illegal arrivals, all to vote Democrat. They have turned California Democrat blue, Nevada, Arizona and New Mexico. Their target, the big target, is Texas. Turned blue, perhaps, with fake elections too."

"No way I will ever, ever vote for President Brandon or any Democrat now that I understand. I have no idea why anyone would do so."

Wilbur said one word, "Money."

Wilbur decided to say more. "I am Latino. Some coming across the border are Latino too and poor, but they revolt against this nonsense. They love the country, their family, their religion and they work hard. Most are honest and like peace and quiet in the streets, not crime."

"Frankly, the Democrats make a mistake with the Latinos. They think we are just like all the other poor, we are not. Still, many Democrats live in the east, where people are not so smart, and in Chicago too. They are sort of backyard."

Rashid asked, "Men and women all buy into this nonsense?"

"For sure," Wilbur answered. "But that may be changing as President Brandon and the Democrats are telling parents and women that they have no say in their children's education. They even put the FBI on them to investigate and jail parents who disagree."

"Our women are too smart to be for President Brandon and the Democrats."

Ramin cut in, "So, is this FBI dishonest? Why go after parents who actually do pay tax? They pay for the schools?"

It was Aziz who answered. "No, the FBI is corrupt. The police arm of the President and the Democrats, hunting down parents that disagree, truckers and working people who oppose their views. Anyone who is a patriot, believes in free speech, no censorship, wants a say in children's future, believes in law and order, equal justice, and opportunity for all."

"Anyone who supported Trump's Wall on the border, the trespassers in DC, who demonstrated for President Trump last year – they are all targets of the FBI. Many of them political prisoners, by that I mean they have been locked up for over a year with no trial, when the rules say everyone has a right to trial in 90 days. But, for your safety, speak nothing of this outside of here."

"Right amigos, say nothing," said Wilbur, "the Democrats only let violent criminals out of jail, not ordinary people. Now get on your way to the bank and cash my checks."

Heading out the door, a big man, Mr. Campos stopped them. "Just a minute. I heard all of that and let me tell you, I am from Venezuela. This is how it started there – give you bags of beans and rice, later a stipend, like these Tax Refunds. They tell you what to do – carry this Chavista card or no medical care, vote for whom they say, get that blue ink on your finger, or lose everything, go to the supermercado only when they permit, and attend a rally for the President or else. The Chavista Point System monitors obedience. People can starve for all they care if they do not cooperate. You just saw in Canada, no, the same thing showed its ugly face. It is coming here too."

"Thank you, Mr. Campos, we know. Can you please sit down and sign your tax report? I have a real refund check for you too," said Wilbur.

Aziz grabbed up Rashid and said, "OK, thank you Wilbur. We will go. We are running late."

To Chaste Bank. In no time, Ramin, Rashid and Hamid had opened bank accounts, got temporary debit cards, and had money in the bank.

"Thank you, Aziz. Thank you too, Mrs. Ball, the banker, for all the help. We are eternally grateful," said Ramin.

They all shook hands, although these new refugees were not used to shaking hands with a woman. It felt funny. They headed back to the LaQuinta, to share their story.

Rashid asked Aziz, "Dine with us, please. We are all hungry. How much do we owe you?"

"You owe me nothing, but I am starving, so I will accept your invitation. Sounds good."

Chapter 14

Having called ahead, everyone at the LaQuinta had prayed and were ready for dinner. They were downstairs, waiting to meet Aziz in the lobby to chat, mostly small talk. The ladies and children were happy to make a new friend in Aziz who repeated, "Please, everyone, put my name and telephone in your phones. Faisil too. In case of emergencies, call."

After a short while dinner was served. It was Beef Stroganoff, with carrots, beans and salad. It was good. The guest finished every morsel. "Thank you and thanks to God. That was delicious and very tasty."

During dinner, the wives were informed about the day's events including how lucky they were to be in America, having bank accounts and being what they call Taxpayers.

Aslan thought all of this very strange. "I cannot really get my mind around these events, but I accept it all. Surely, it does not exist anyplace else on earth."

Aziz asked for coffee after dinner, instead of tea, and was going to smoke a cigarette but no smoking was allowed. Instead, he splurged on a piece of carrot cake.

"This cake is moist and light. Try some, please, children. You will like it."

With that, everyone got a piece of the cake or at least a shared bite. It was unanimous that the cake was great.

Good food, good friends, good conversation. The definition of happiness for over 2,000 years and still true today.

Once upstairs, the unanimous decision was made and Ramin announced it. "Tomorrow, we will leave the LaQuinta and go to our new homes. We can go early and finish cleaning, then move everything in the afternoon."

Excepting, Jamil interjected, "Great, but we must be back for lunch. It is American cheeseburgers. Please, Daddy."

Magi and Mona were all smiles, looking straight at Ramin.

"Of course." Hugs were exchanged by all on this news.

One last item for the night.

Ramin announced to the delight of everyone, "With some of our new money, we will buy three laptops for the ladies. In this way, they can be used for news, education and Online Backgammon."

He knew the women were avid and excellent players. It would be a happy hobby for them during their free time. The men knew they were no competition. Better let them play other champions Online than face defeat at home.

Bed time.

Chapter 15

Moving day had arrived.

Ramin notified Faisil of the plan. He would pick them up early for the morning cleaning and set up, and spend the entire day with them. Yes, including the Jamil cheeseburger lunch.

"Agreed."

"In the morning, we will make room in my truck for everyone. In the afternoon, I will have a friend from the Mosque meet us at the LaQuinta so there will be room for everyone and everything."

"Perfect."

"OK, thank you, Faisil. We shall see you at 8:00 a.m. tomorrow, God willing. We will all be downstairs, waiting for you. Don't pay to park, please."

The rest of the evening was all about washing soiled clothing, packing, making ready for new life. Ramin texted Mr. Everett to notify him of the plans. He approved, saying he would try to visit them the following day at their new homes. All was set.

By the end of the evening all was in readiness. Most things were packed, bathing was all done and the lights were out. Only for Ramin to hear Tamara tell him, "My dear husband, I will miss the convenience of the LaQuinta and the nice people. Later, we must bring them some Turkish Delight as a treat to say thank you, please."

"Pistachio, would that work for you?"

"Yes, thank you, Ramin. I love you so, and I will tell Aslan and Yasmine of our plan. Good night my dearest. Allah maak. How exciting."

"Good night, God's blessings upon you my dear."

At 8:00 a.m. sharp, Faisil was out front sipping a coffee.

"Good morning. Jump in."

It was a scramble, but everyone got onboard. With Pakistani music blaring, of course, away they went.

Ramin had the morning planned. "I will go across the street to Khalil's store. What did he call it, International Foods, to shop for food with Tamara. The children can come too. The rest of you can organize the new apartments. If you need anything, call me."

"Rashid. Hamid. Please help the women and watch over them while I am away."

Faisil parked at the HCA. There was Mrs. Jinx. "Good morning everyone. Welcome. Come through the gate, it's open. We are steam cleaning the walkways. They are wet, be careful."

"Thank you and good day to you, Mrs. Jinx. We are here to finish up for we move in today, this afternoon. If that is permissible?" replied Ramin.

"Yes, great news. We are happy to see all of you. Hello children."

"Hello, Mrs. Jinx. Thank you."

Mrs. Jinx thought to herself, what lovely children, so well behaved. Something she felt was far too rare in Chicago.

"It is Diana's day off, so you will see her later. If you need anything, just holler. I'll be out front."

Tamara had the list of things to buy for the families including some Turkish Delight for everyone, including a gift of it for the staff at the LaQuinta.

Ramin pushed the cart. "Hello Khalil. Best wishes." Faisil spoke with Khalil while the others shopped. "So, Khalil, business is good and you are happy?"

"Thanks to God, yes, all is well. Noor is in the walk-in box organizing our cheese shipment, olives, which are all fresh now. Perfect time to shop. Do you need anything, brother?"

"Yes, I want two dozen pita and one pound of Kalamata olives, please."

"Just one moment, you shall have it. I will send you some Baklava too. Noor just made it yesterday and it is delicious."

"Thank you. You are a good friend indeed. I love that sweet temptation."

"Here, Faisil, is a nice sweet tea. Let's enjoy it while our brothers and sisters shop. Here children, please share these Jordan Almonds. Give some to Ramin and Tamara too."

"Thank you, these are sooo good. OK."

"Khalil, we forgot about these little gems. Please give us one pound," said Ramin. The little snack was hard to resist.

After a while, Tamara had collected two shopping carts full of rice, lentils, sugar, honey, flour, dry yeast, corn starch, corn syrup, okra, string beans, tomato sauce, olive oil, wine vinegar, garbanzo beans, lemon, spices of all sorts, butter, plain yogurt, Cherios, bulgar wheat, at least three cheeses, dozens of pita bread, eggs, milk, coffee, tea, greens, onions, cucumbers, Persian cucumbers, pickles, eggplant, lamb, six lamb heads, chicken, organic chicken deli slices, cans of ready-made grape leaves, and bottles of grape leaves as well. Cabbage, carrots, turnips, celery, potatoes, pasta and cheese pizzas, per Jamil's request. Paper products, toothpaste, dental floss, bandages, ointments, matches, three ibeks to make Turkish coffee, hot chocolate powder for the children, and several kinds of nuts. They even bought some tuna to try, as they had enjoyed it at LaQuinta. They also bought mayo, mustard, ketchup, several hot chilis and chili sauce, club soda. Upon inspecting fruits, they bought dates, apples, oranges, frozen berries, raisins, melon, and lots of dried figs and apricots.

"We cannot leave without the Syrian apricots," Ramin was saying, pointing to the flat-wrapped delicacy.

"In that case, my husband, can we afford some Baklava as well, everyone enjoys it with tea. Please."

"Of course. I heard Khalil say Noor just made it. Please pick up a tray, and we will feast."

"Thank you. Oh my, I have to ask her to show me how to make this. I really do not know."

It cost $420.56 for everything. Ramin called out, "Thank you Khalil. We shall see you, God willing, soon. We will go now and stock our homes with your fine foods. We hope to move in this afternoon with God's help, Faisil's, and our friend from our Mosque."

"Ramin, is that allot of money? Is it OK? I am sorry if I got too much."

"No Tamara, this is expected. Thankfully, we have the money from our America friends. Soon, I shall go to work. We are fine and life is good."

"I love you, Ramin, you know that?"

"Yes, my dear wife, I love you too, and the children. I love all of you."

"I love all of you too, even Khalil," Faisil said with a hearty laugh. "All ready, then, let's go. We have work to do. Khalil, best wishes to Noor."

Magi and the children remembered to say goodbye and thank you. Khalil was very impressed, they were kind, polite and well raised. He thought, a bit of fresh air in Chicago.

Unloading the shopping to upstairs was a chore. Soon enough everything was distributed by the women as planned.

It was decided there would be communal dinner for the entire group, all in one apartment, starting with Aslan's home, to rotate weekly between them. The three women also discussed what to prepare.

Rashid overheard the conversation. "Great ideas, ladies. Very well, we shall start in our apartment. Now, we will go back to the LaQuinta for lunch, to pack, and to say our goodbyes."

"Ramin, let's go at 2:00 p.m. A brother from the Mosque will join us to help move you to your new homes. Let's go man."

Rashid gave a hug to Faisil, who was somewhat taken aback, and off they went, windows down, music up.

Rashid said, "Bye Mrs. Jinx, we shall see you this afternoon."

"See you later, I will be here."

No matter the smiles and the music that filled the cabin, there was a general sense of apprehension, maybe even fear, so Faisil spoke. "I have helped others come here. I came here 12 years ago. It was different then. It is OK to feel a little scared now that you moved away from the sanctuary of LaQuinta, into the real world. Everything is different – people, places and language. Have faith in Allah. He shows us the way forward."

Rashid looked around. Everyone agreed. "This is true, but we shall do what is necessary. If we do not do what is needed, we will not be doing God's work."

"Well put, Rashid, you always have the smartest thing to say," said Ramin.

Faisil thought about it and summed it up. "It is not what we did or what we knew in the past. It is not what we will do or what we will know in the future. It is what we will do and think within us, in our minds' as God provides his wisdom."

Aslan understood. "Yes, we must accept, rejoice and trust in God. Allah Akbar."

Back at the LaQuinta for the last time, all the rooms were cleaned, things packed, short prayers said and then off to the cheeseburger lunch.

"Girls," Aslan said, "we shall all wear masks, to school too. Everyone, OK. I spoke to my husband, and we agree, as long as your hair is short, you will not need to cover it. You will more easily fit in."

"We don't mind at all. We are accustomed to it and it is right," answered Mona.

"Well, I did not say it correctly. It is up to you and how you feel comfortable. We have no objection, and the Prophet, praise be unto him, did say in a strange land it is OK not to draw attention to yourself."

"OK, Mommy." It was settled.

Lunch, which no one seemed to know why, was more delicious than ever. "Reuben, this is the best ever. We will miss you all very much. We would like to give you this gift of Turkish Delight to share, from all of us," said Rashid.

"Thank you. So you are leaving, when, today?"

"Yes, after lunch, but we will always remember all of you. We hope to see you soon, God willing. Stay well."

Soft serve ice cream was brought out by Reuben for the entire group. "OK, so long, and enjoy the ice cream. Chocolate swirl is my favorite," he said.

"Thank you."

It was the best ever.

Chapter 16

Farhad arrived exactly at 2:00 p.m. Faisil saw him in the lobby at once. "Hello Farhad, come meet our new family."

The customary, never-ending greetings followed. Everyone was finally in the lift off to their rooms to clean up and collect their belongings. Then to head to the awaiting trucks. "Here, let me help you, Aslan," said Farhad as he took a heavy bag from her. "Come follow me to my truck. We will make a couple trips."

The scene was repeated in all three rooms as everything was taken downstairs taking two trips, somethings three, up and down. But with five men to help, it went fast.

"Thank you so much, both of you and God's Blessings upon you. Such great friends to help us," said Aslan.

Farhad answered, "Most welcome, Ramin. Maybe you can go upstairs one last time to check to see if you have left anything behind, please. We will wait."

"Good idea. Come Rashid and Hamid, let's be thorough."

"Faisil, may I ride with Farhad, please? I want to see what his Ram is like."

"Sure Jamil, tell your dad when he gets back. Maybe Rashid's family goes with you and the rest ride with me."

"That sounds fine."

A short time after the trucks rolled out of LaQuinta, the HCA was in sight. Jamil exclaim, "Farhad, your truck is so cool. Oh, there's our new home," pointing to the HCA.

He was right. There they were, Mrs. Jinx and Diana, chatting while waiting for their arrival as to help out.

"Hello Mrs. Jinx, Diana, so kind of you. We are fine. We only have some personal belongings to take upstairs," said Tamara.

"Welcome. We are here to help, right, Mrs. Jinx?"

"Right, Diana, so let's get to work and get my new tenants comfy."

With one trip up, all arms full, everything was delivered. Everyone smiled, hugged, "Thank you, Mrs. Jinx, this is great," said Aslan. "Thank you, Diana."

"OK, we will let you all get settled in. You have our numbers so call anytime. Bye for now." Diana joined Mrs. Jinx, "Yes, see you all soon." The ladies made their way out.

"We are off as well, Farhad and I, to the Mosque for afternoon prayers. You guys stay put, stay safe, and enjoy your new homes, God willing."

That started the traditional goodbye ritual, lasting about 15 minutes, with hugs, pats on the back, and good wishes. Everyone was in Ramin's apartment. With the goodbyes said, everyone finally got a chance to sit down and embrace each other in the moment with cups of tea.

The women were fidgety wanting to get started with dinner. But Hamid had other ideas. "Brothers and sisters, and children, go wash up. We will go across to the Crescent for dinner. I called and arranged it. You worked enough today."

Rashid was very happy. He could see Aslan was tired too. "Great idea, let us go now, while there is still daylight."

Everyone was out the door in a flash of excitement.

Sara greeted them at the door. Akbar was in the kitchen. "Please come in. Everything is ready. Sit here, please. How nice to see all of you."

"I ordered when I called. Let us give thanks to Allah and enjoy."

"We have the meal prepared, Hamid, should I serve it now?"

"Please do and thank you. There is something for everyone, especially the children, like a double order of Chicken Tikka."

"That's a yes from us," said Magi and Mona.

"Sounds great." Jamil asked Hamid, "Anything else?"

"Well, there is Biryani." Jamil burst in, "Fantastic, I almost forgot about it."

"And Seekh Kababs, Samosas and Channa Chaat. We need veggies, right?"

"And, lots of Hot Rice with carrot and raisins."

Yasmine looked at Hamid with a smile. "You have done wonderful. Is there anything sweet?"

Hamid knew his wife's taste, "Yes, yes, Halva Pri. I know you like it."

That brought a smile to everyone's face. "Thank you Hamid, for remembering."

Ramin told Hamid, "The three men will pay. Let us now enjoy a family style meal."

Drinks were already on the table including Doogh, Persian Pomegranate, Tea, as was small plates of carrots, radishes, onion, cucumber, spices, hot sauce, a bounty of plain yogurt, and hot bread from the oven.

Magi spoke for everyone when she exclaimed, "Oh, Daddy,

this is so much like back home."

Everyone agreed, as the food arrived, bringing beautiful plates and familiar aromas to the table.

"Rashid, my dear husband, may we arrange to take a small plate to Mrs. Jinx and Diana? They have been so wonderful to us."

"They will get some of everything. We shall enjoy, by the grace of God, today."

"No worry," said Hamid, "I ordered enough for Farhad and Faisil too, but they went to prayers. So we have plenty to share. Let's eat and not worry."

The food was hot, tasteful, and as close to home cooking as it gets.

Sara made a few trips, "Here are extra plates so you can eat family style and share, like back home."

The hit of the evening, as usual, was the Chicken Tikka. Fresh, hot, spiced just right – the double order barely met demand.

"Hmmmmm, good," Jamil was heard saying.

"Better than that cheeseburger, son?"

"Yes, Daddy, thank you."

This time it was Khalil who spoke, "The food is good. So happy you came. Here are boxes and sacks for the food to go. Children, was the food all to your taste?"

Magi, "Oh, yes, thank you." Mona said the same. Jamil said, "Wow," with a noticeable twinkle in his eye.

After some more tea, the bill was settled. The to go boxes were packed, and it was time to head home before it was late.

"Good night, Khalil and Sara. It was the best. We hope to see you again soon, inish Allah," said Aslan. Everyone repeated the same thing, with lots of hugs, smiles and peace.

It was nearly dark by the time the group arrived back at the HCA. Mrs. Jinx was watering her roses.

"Hello Mrs. Jinx. We have come from the Crescent and am bringing you and Diana plates of the most delicious foods. Please enjoy," said Yasmine.

"Oh, thank you. We love their cooking. Bet you ordered your favorites, right?"

Yasmine nodded her head, "So true."

"Welcome home. Now you can feel secure, have a roof over your head, sleep in your own beds and get into a normal routine again."

Everyone within earshot grasped the idea. Finally they had arrived. Thanks to God.

"Yes, Mrs. Jinx, we are very grateful, relieved and more relaxed knowing we have a home and you and Diana being so close. Thank you."

"Don't mention it. sleep well, Yasmine, everyone. I will go in now to sample these treats. I will give Diana her plate tomorrow."

The apartments were warm and quiet. Light conversation swirled around life ahead as everyone got ready for the first night's sleep away from the sanctuary of the LaQunita.

Tomorrow was to be a day dedicated to the children. Everyone would go together to the Elgin School to admit them. This was decided during dinner.

The children were apprehensive, but Aslan had reassured them, "Just be yourself, be proud, and be thankful to God for the chance to learn. Study is the important thing."

Ramin had cut one of Mrs. Jinx's roses, put it in a bottle and gave it to Tamara. "God bless you and the children," he said, "We shall make the best of it."

Tamara hugged Ramin like only a wife could hug her husband of many years.

"Lights out, everyone."

Chapter 17

The next morning's walk past the Elgin Park and to Elgin School was pleasant. The cool breeze was refreshing.

Upon entering the school, the three men remained in the hallway while Aslan and Tamara got the children enrolled, one by one. Yasmine helped with the paperwork including vaccinations, identification and hand written notes on each student's past level of education.

Jamil, qualified for 3rd Grade, Magi for 4th Grade and Mona for 5th Grade. Each one was walked over to their home room class to meet the teachers, say hello to the class, and start learning. Parents walked about halfway, waived and watched as their children started their new life in America.

It was good the children had attended English School back home. Their English was good, and they were actually a little more advanced than their new peers.

"We can go now, all is well. They have snacks. The school has water fountains. We will pick them up at 2:00 p.m. by the flag pole and the children know," said Ramin.

Tamara heard, "Yes, everyone is aware that we meet at the flag pole. We can go home now. Maybe we can stop in the park for a moment."

It was nearly 11:00 a.m. by the time they reached Elgin Park. The gardens, flowers and trees were beautiful. The children's play area was newly washed with the water driving at least a dozen homeless men off the apparatus.

"So many homeless, I don't understand," said Aslan. "These poor people are everyplace. We saw many driving with Faisil. They are all poor and rents are so high. Who can afford to pay. Many are drug addicts and criminals too."

Ramin knew she was right, "Remember to carry the pocket knife I bought each of you. The self-defense pepper spray I ordered for you arrives soon."

All admired the beauty of the park, yet they felt a danger lurking and caution was the word.

Back at the HCA, "What a pleasant surprise," said Tamara. "Look, there is Mrs. Jinx and Diana. It must be her day off."

Mrs. Jinx saw Tamara and the others, "Good morning, Tamara, first day of school for the children always exciting, right?"

"Yes, very exciting. The school is very modern and clean, and the staff we met were very helpful. We hope the children will fall in love with education."

"You pick them up by 2:00 p.m., you know?"

"Yes, we will all go and collect them. Hello Diana. Is this your day off?"

"Right, no work for me today, just gardening which is not work. You see our lovely roses?"

"Yes, and I apologize, I have one at home. A gift from you, made by my lovely husband, who could not resist pinching one for me. Thank you."

Ramin smiled and Diana took note. "Ramin, how nice. We can cut more from those over there for your apartments."

Hamid was already on the way along with Mrs. Jinx. "Yes, one each for Aslan and my darling Yasmine?"

Done, with smiles all around.

Rashid was curious to know what Diana did at the police department. They chatted, and Diana looked to the group and said, "For over four years. I am in Police Intel, trying to get a hold on the gangs and violent crime that you see on the news. It is a pandemic of crime, bigger than COVID-19 and killing more people than ever. It is important work and the team under me has six members. We do our best."

Rashid asked, "Has it always been this bad?"

"No, it is getting worse, no matter what the police do. The Aldermen and the Mayor are for defunding the police. So we have no budget and anti-police policies put fear into officers on the beat. No one vigorously enforces the law for fear of getting fired."

"Really."

"It is worse than that. When we do catch criminals, even killers, the prosecutor does not want to press charges. The Judges are asked to release them without bail so they can kill again. Most people we arrest are out on their own recognizance having committed many other crimes or violated probation. No one cares. The gangs know it and take advantage of it. I make reports all the time on the situation to the political class but never get a reply."

Ramin cut in, "The gangs are responsible for most crime, so how many are there?"

"About 120,000 gang members in Chicago. Anytime a student drops out of high school, he or she flunks a gang. Flunking is the only admission requirement. In the good old days they got drafted into the Army and gained self-respect. There are black gangs, white gangs, Chinese, Vietnamese, Latino, Polish, Jewish, Irish, Italian, Russian, Ukrainian, Anarchist, and even gangs of perverts and pedophiles."

"What sort of crime?"

"Ramin, crime and violence come in all forms. Kidnapping,

carjacking, robbery, murder for hire, extortion and protection, gambling, sex crimes, drugs, and arson, you name it. The gang wars are about drug turf and hundreds die due to it."

"Do you get any help from anyone else?"

"We get help from the Feds, DEA, AFT and FBI. But when did you see anyone arrested by FBI agents unless talking about pro Trump citizens, just arrested for political opinion? They really do nothing to help."

"That is amazing, we had corruption back home but nothing like this."

"Corruption, city politics, sanctuary city policies – all promote recidivist crime. Like when we arrest an illegal alien or say a killer, and we release him pre-trial, even if the U.S. Immigration Service or ICE has a hold on him, a Detainer, asking us to turn the wanted fugitive over to them. But we cannot cooperate. We are forced to release him and the guy probably kills again."

Rashid heard and understood every word. His language skills being superb, he said, "You must be very frustrated with your work."

"I just do my job. If others don't, nothing will ever change it. My colleagues and I work, hoping to get our pension and get out. That is the ticket."

Ramin pointed his finger toward the sky, "Be safe in your work. If we can help in any way, please ask. We are honest people and we shall pray to Allah to assist you in making Chicago safe again."

Diana rolled her eyes, "That may be harder than Making America Great Again."

"No worry, Diana. Allah can do both, I promise you."

Hamid asked Diana, "Did you like the plate of food we sent?"

"My goodness, yes. I forgot to say thank you – thank you, delicious. I have to find out more about your cuisine."

"There is much more to our cooking than that and we shall share with you – what it is, how it tastes, and how to cook and serve it, right Tamara?" said Aslan.

Tamara smiled broadly and nodded in happy agreement.

After a short time, working in and talking about the garden, it became time to return to Elgin School to the flag pole to meet the children.

The streets around the school were clogged with cars and vans of parents picking up their children. Soon enough the gates opened and out ran dozens, if not hundreds of children, each homing in on the awaiting vehicles.

A few other parents were on foot, and as one might guess, the flag pole was the common meeting place. It was crowded with amiable people and little children. The sound of so many happy children – its noise was uplifting, fresh and pure fun. One by one, Jamil, Magi and Mona appeared out of the masses, each had a smile upon their face.

Yasmine observed, "Look, how beautiful – all three with smiles – the day must have been good."

It was like a grand reunion, everyone together under the waving red, white and blue. Hugs, smiles and lots of pictures were taken at this first day of school. A new start.

"Mommy, we are hungry. We had lunch, but the food was different," said Jamil. The girls joined in saying, "exactly."

"OK, let's walk home. You can tell us all about your day. We can have some hot rice and left overs from yesterday while they are still fresh," answered Tamara.

"Great."

As the children were hungry, they were told to pray with their fathers, wash and make ready for an early dinner. Everyone sat together and learned about the day.

The community dinner in Ramin's apartment was readied by the three women. The table looked inviting, especially the rice that Tamara had doctored up and extended by adding some of her secret ingredients.

The conversation was more interesting than the adults expected, starting with Jamil.

"Yes, Daddy, the day was very cool. I mean different and we studied words and spelling, a lot. We said the Pledge of Allegiance to the Flag. The kids know it by memory."

Mona butted in, "Yes, us too. We said Pledge Allegiance to the Flag, One Nation Under God, for everyone is equal."

Jamil went on to talk about a woman who came to class and talked about sex.

Rashid said, "Jamil don't make things up, this is not possible."

Ramin looked at his brother, "Jamil does not make things up. Let him speak and tell everyone. Jamil, now."

"Well, Daddy, I did not understand. It was about how a boy can wear girl clothing, and a girl can wear boy clothing, and how doctors can change boys and girls. All you have to do is go see the school Nurse."

Everything stopped at the table, dead silence.

Jamil was only eight years old and had no idea about the birds and the bees, his brain would not finish growing until he was in his mid-20s. They all realized something was strange indeed.

Ramin managed to take the initiative.

"Jamil, do you know the name of this woman?"

"No Daddy."

"OK, do you want to be a girl, my son?"

"No, Daddy."

"Did any classmate want to be a girl?"

"No, Daddy, but one girl said she wanted to be a boy."

"What happened?"

"I don't know, she left with the woman."

"You believe this person talking to you was a woman?"

"Yes, Daddy."

"Magi, Mona, did this same thing happen to you today?"

Mona answered, "Yes Uncle, the woman came to our classes too and said the same thing, but no one understood or really listened."

Ramin looked at his wife, Tamara, and asked, "Do you have something to say, please?

That is all Tamara had to hear. "Look at me children, look at us. This woman is abnormal and what she says is against Allah. It is contradictory to the teachings of the Prophet, praise be unto him. As you grow up, you will be presented with lies, with evil, and with temptation which is the devil shytan's work. You must trust in Allah, keep your faith, and thank Allah for your good fortune. There are only two types of people in the world Allah made for us, Boys and Girls. There is no change before Allah."

Here comes Aslan, "Magi, Mona, you are my children. Allah gave you life as girls, and you are girls. Jamil, Allah gave you life as a boy. You are a boy for life and soon will be a man, here and in heaven beyond. Turn your face away from this evil teaching that only destroys the people who follow it."

It was now Ramin's turn to speak.

"You have heard the wise words of your mothers and I thank them. Now I tell you, Jamil, Magi and Mona, trust in Allah. Be not afraid and stand up for yourself for being a boy or girl as Allah has decided. Do not fight Allah but fight those who would break you down. Do not be timid to say your beliefs – we are not timid. Do you understand?"

All three children got the picture. Ramin was stern and they were used to that, but in this moment, he was intense. They got the message. There was no tolerance for such minds.

Aslan, again, said to her girls, "Mona, Magi, you like being girls?"

"Yes, Mommy, we love being girls. We want to be like you."

"Inish Allah, you shall be. OK, eat before the food is cold. Jamil, eat like a man and grow strong, God willing."

Soon dinner was done and everyone were heading back to their apartments. The adults agreed to talk to Mrs. Jinx about the strange happenings of the day. This was new to them and it repelled them at every level of their being.

Ramin decided for the others not to go to work a couple more days. They would repeat today's routine again tomorrow and do some recon to better understand the locale. He also wanted to know who this woman was at the school.

The next day was much the same, no big surprises, except learning the school teaches reading, and writing in only printing, not cursive. That seemed strange because writing and calligraphy were important aspects of all art back home – throughout the near, middle, and far east, but no longer in the west.

Rashid wondered how these children would learn to sign their names in English. Perhaps, they never would.

Rashid asked, "Children, do you have homework?"

Mona answered for them, "No Daddy, we don't get homework."

"Do you have any books? I don't see any."

"No Daddy we do not use books, only i-tablets on the desk, no books."

"I see, so no writing, no homework, and no books. I am happy this school is free, unlike how we paid back home. But it is lacking – it is important for all of you to attend school at the Mosque on the weekends or you may never learn anything of value."

"Yes, Daddy, we want to go to the Mosque and School. We can make friends there."

"So be it, inish Allah."

Dinner tonight was peasant food and delicious. It consisted of lentils and rice, yogurt, olives, eggplant, bread, a big salad with olive oil and lemon, pistachios and beverages. Conversation was simple.

"We learned geography too, Mommy," Jamil said out loud and the girls agreed. "Today, we had maps of India, Pakistan, and of the mountains of our home. No one knew the names of any of those places, but I did. I pointed out our city."

Ramin liked this. "Very good, children, all of you make us proud. We know it is not easy for you. Keep up the good work and tell your mother about any problems."

"Yes."

Looking at his wife, he went on, "We will continue with these activities. Rashid and I will go to our first day's work. Hamid does not have to report until next week. He will accompany you to school, to the store, and with whatever you may need."

"Thank you, Ramin, I will do so, God willing. Yasmine proposes we go shopping before picking up the children, if OK, so we can make lamb heads and shanks. I crave them."

That was a hit with everybody. They all agreed. After some light tea, everyone was off to bed.

No matter the stresses of life, it was true, planning a good meal, then having it, spelled relief for one and all. Lamb heads, what a good idea.

Chapter 18

The next morning, Hamid went along with the women and children to Elgin School. Arriving early, the children literally ran into the entrance. When they turned to go home, they saw Diana and another woman and a child.

"Good morning, Tamara and Aslan. It's nice to see you. Are the children liking school?"

"Hello Diana," replied Tamara, "you can see they run to school, very excited. Who is your friend, if I may ask?"

"Tamara, Aslan, Hamid, this is Jennie, my dear friend, and her little girl, Amy. She is seven years old and in the 2nd Grade."

Jennie had just gotten little Amy into the school. "Hi, nice to meet you. I hear so much about you from Diana. Welcome to Chicago."

Hamid was now surrounded by five women and he figured someone had the answer to his question. "May I ask, what is this that the children tell us about a woman asking boys to become girls and vice versa? Do you know?"

Jennie gave a sigh, rolled her eyes, and replied, "Hamid, it is Hamid, right? This is the Democrats and President Brandon, again, trying to force their narrative, their propaganda into the schools and onto our children at a very young age."

Now, Aslan was tuned in, "Please explain."

"As everyone knows, there is a gay population in America. They have equal rights with non-gay people. That is wonderful, having no discrimination based on sexual preference. At the same time, some people are transvestites which are men who like to wear women's clothing. Some people are transexuals, now being called transgender which means they want hormones and operations to change sex. We do not discriminate against them either. Now, President Brandon and the Democrats want to increase the size of this tiny minority, so they push sex change in the schools to the children, going so far as giving hormones without parental consent. These people seem crazy - groom kids in school, exclude parents, and make taxpayers pay for it."

Aslan and the others were shocked. "But why target children?"

"Because they are vulnerable and the Democrats control the school administration and school boards so they force the issue. Parents try to fight back by attending PTA. I do, you know, and parents want to have a voice in the matter. It is their tax dollars that pay for the schools, right?"

"Good."

"But, the school police and President Brandon's Federal Bureau of Investigation come to intimidate, even arrest the parents. They're saying they have no voice in the education of their children. It doesn't matter that they pay the bills out of their property and sales taxes."

Diana did not miss a word. "You heard her, the school police and the FBI, not your local Police. No way, we do not agree. We do not enforce this sort of nonsense. It is the Democrats and the FBI, the Federal power, not us."

"I thought the FBI fought terrorism?"

"Not any more," said Diana, with Jennie in full agreement. "Today the FBI has hundreds of agents investigating parents, and investigating the Capital Riot of January 6, 2021. Also hundreds investigating patriots who oppose the socialist takeover of the United States and those who want a secure border from drug traffic and illegal aliens."

"This is corrupt to me. It is all wrong," said Hamid.

"There is corruption, many people now see the FBI as new world order Gestapo of President Brandon. Citizens it arrested have been in jail for two years with no trial and in complete violation of the Constitution. The major media, tech companies, and Democrats, they don't care at all."

Hamid had to ask, "What about your elections, they do no good?"

Jennie answered, "Fake elections, President Brandon's win was not entirely legit. He lost all 27 major counties in the USA that one needs to win, but he won anyway due to events in several key States. It is obvious. The major media, tech companies, and rich Democratic donors, even from abroad, make sure that the electronic and paper vote is questionable. People know it. What can they do? If you open your mouth, the FBI accuses you of treason and arrests you to cement the power of President Brandon and the Democrats. You cannot say a word, so don't quote me, please."

"Is this new in America?" asked Tamara.

Diana replied, "It is new with major media, tech companies, and the Federal government melted together into what Hitler had with his business class and Paul Joseph Goebbels in charge. It is National Fascism, we called them Nazis, this is the same. News is fake, so are elections, and everything is propaganda, making Goebbels very proud of the Democrats, for sure."

Yasmine wondered, "OK, what can we do?"

Diana told her, "Go with Jennie to the next PTA or School Board Meeting, but be prepared to be surprised. It is a fight for freedom fought by forlorn parents."

"Ok, Jennie, we will go with you. Here are our cell numbers on this paper. We support you. We have no fear, Allah accompanies us."

The group walked back to the HCA. Jennie was to spend the day with Diana. Others were off to make a feast of lamb heads. Aslan insisted, "You must come, all three of you, and join us for dinner at my apartment at 6:00 p.m. Invite Mrs. Jinx too."

"Deal," said Diana. "We are both off today and we will be there. I will take Jennie home in my squad car, no problem."

"We all eat together and I will add four plates, so there will be 13 of us, including Mrs. Jinx. How fun."

It was settled and the idea of having friends over was simply thrilling.

Aslan's cell phone rang.

"Hello Rashid, my darling. Is all well? OK, fine. Yes, I invited Diana and her friend Jennie to dinner tonight. No, we shall get everything we need. Dinner will be served at 6:00 p.m., inish Allah, don't be late."

Shopping for food was done by 11:00 a.m. The preparation ensued, and was made ready for the big feast, except the final cooking before the 2:00 p.m. pick up. A couple of lamb shanks were purchased just in case the guests were not keen on heads.

The air was fresh and the walk from HCA to school was pleasant. The voices of children playing carried upon the cool breeze. Sure enough, at 2:00 p.m., the three tots appeared with smiles. They wanted to stop at the park to play but there was no time. They had the feast to prepare.

Back at the HCA, there was a frenzy of cleaning, prayers, another table, more chairs, final cooking preparation, and everything was made ready for dinner. The spread was beautiful and the aroma, wow!

Thankfully by 5:30 p.m. everyone was home. Ramin and Rashid shared their stories about their first day at work. There was no time for details because guests were arriving for dinner.

Hamid answered the door at 6:00 p.m. Before he could say a word, Diana announced that Mrs. Jinx could not come. Diana went on to say, "Maybe we can save something to send back for her?"

"Welcome, Come in, yes, do. Please take off your shoes. Everyone, meet Jennie and her daughter, Amy."

It was a small apartment with a big crowd around the guests.

Aslan motioned everyone in. "If you wish to wash your hands, the bathroom is over there. As you can see, everything is ready. I am sorry it is not more."

Anyone who has ever enjoyed a meal in the home of a Moslem brother or sister knows full well everything is put out. Nothing is held back. Eat, drink and rejoice in the grace of Allah.

Diana's blue eyes were big and round, "More, no way, this will feed an army."

"Good thing," Jennie said, "I am starved and this all looks fabulous, right, Amy?"

Hamid, hugged Yasmine, and broadcast the news, "Lamb heads and shanks for Yasmine's birthday. I have hidden away in my room a tray of Shakila Baklava for dessert."

"Happy birthday and many more."

Ramin took charge. "Please to sit down and thanks to Allah for the food, the family, the friends, and the love. Let us eat. Happy Birthday, Yasmine."

No masks, no hair covering, not at home, no matter the guests. Only glittering eyes, pleasant smiles, and thanks to Allah all around.

Rashid and Aslan sat at the head of the table. The hosts marveled at how much little Amy liked the food. Her mother was surprised as well, "She is usually a picky eater, but not tonight."

Dinner was a hit. There was a big plate set aside for Mrs. Jinx.

Amy, Magi, Mona, even Jamil, sitting on the same side of the table, were all smiles. It was beautiful.

Tea, coffee, and Baklava followed in honor of Yasmine and her birthday.

No questions asked. All 12 diners loved the dessert. Who wouldn't – the Shakila Bakery – there is none better.

As Diana drove Jennie and Amy home, she shared her thoughts about their new Afghani women friends. "I have to tell you, I sort of don't get it."

"What?"

"The women are timid outdoors, cover up hair and skin, yet, at home, wow, they are like in control. They talk and the men listen, they drink coffee, smoke cigarettes, and they seem very tough. It just surprises me."

"I got that feeling too. I think women in the Islamic world are just like anyone else and very tough cookies. Their religion teaches them the virtue of modesty and humility when outside."

"I think we will learn more about this reality soon enough."

"Sounds right," answered Diana. "There is your apartment, OK. Good night, Amy. I am glad you had a good time. I see that you got some left overs too."

"Yes, for tomorrow. It's sooo good. Good night."

Once back at the HCA, Diana dropped the big plate off for Mrs. Jinx. They agreed it was nice to have new friends and Diana headed to bed. She had an early work call in the morning.

Chapter 19

The next day was pretty routine. Ramin and Rashid went to work. Hamid, with Yasmine, accompanied the others to and from school. They had time to stop by the park for child's play.

While in the park with the children, Rashid called Aslan to tell her his job was going well. He would work out of an office a few blocks from home instead of downtown. He would be home by 5:00 p.m. on office days and work from home two days a week.

Aslan shared this news.

"That is great," said Tamara. "Ramin's security company is close by and I know he will work most weekends so he can be free for some of the school days."

"Same," said Hamid. "No schedule now, but any day could be a work day for me as a new hire, usually afternoons, even nights, so I should be around too, inish Allah."

That was all good to hear.

By late afternoon, everyone had regrouped at the HCA to clean up, pray and gather in Rashid's apartment for community dinner. Great left overs again and a different fabulous rice and crispy, buttery bun.

Just as tea and more Baklava was being dished out, Faisil knocked at the door.

"Hello there you all. It's me and Farhad. How are things?"

Everyone was on their feet, Aslan too. "Come in, come in, perfect timing," said Tamara, "please more plates and cups for our guest."

Faisil answered, "No, we just ate at the Crescent, but we can't say no to dessert."

Rashid pointed to two empty chairs, "Good, welcome, and please sit down."

It somehow felt familiar, like back home.

"Friday at 5:00 p.m., Farhad and I will come to take everyone to the Mosque for services. Saturday morning as well, for the children's school. How does that sound?"

Aslan answered for everyone. "Thanks to Allah and thank you both. We cannot wait to join you. We long to attend services with our brothers and sisters in Islam, God willing."

She went on, "Farhad, do you have family, to bring too?"

"No, I have no family here as yet."

"Not true, Farhad, all of us," gesturing to the gathering. "All of us are your family and you are part of our family. You too Faisil, you know that already."

"Thank you."

"You are welcome and to you both, we take dinner at 6:30 p.m. Please come every day. We await you."

"Thank you, again,"

Rashid echoed what she said and everyone knew Aslan was right. There was love in the group for one another.

For the next several days, all things were pretty much routine. There were no colds or flu. Community dinner was soon to be moved to Tamara's apartment, which Aslan rather appreciated.

Hamid started work, as an administrative tech in the office, dispatching EMTs, doing paperwork, and following emergencies around the city. His schedule ran from Wednesday to Sunday, 2:00 p.m. to 10:00 p.m., so he was home every morning and off Monday and Tuesday.

Rashid now worked away from home two days a week.

Only Ramin was away Monday - Friday, 9:00 a.m. to 5:00 p.m. mostly doing retail store security, as a lead in toward better work.

Hamid would miss the Friday services at the Mosque, as he had to work, but he would join the others on Saturday. Since starting the job, he sounded more and more like Ramin. Be careful here, be careful there, it got to be monotonous.

They knew he was right. Rashid brought over a dozen old newspapers, the Tribunal, and got a new one every day. None were ever thrown away because they provided news, fashion, cooking, sports, and more, and became a great way to practice English, especially for the children.

He always brought home copies of the Final Caller, the newspaper of the Nation of Moslem, as it reported on much of the same news but in new and provocative ways. He never failed to purchase the paper from the respectable men selling them in the street.

Rashid could readily see these Moslems loved Allah, family, education, hard work, and honesty. The people who disliked the paper never read it, but to him, working in the press was both an obligation and a pleasure to read and share it at home.

Some of the news was worrisome, and the adults tried to keep it out of the children's sight. But they read it too, like:

Retirement Home Attacked, Robbed, Residents and Staff Reported Dead

27th Post Person Robbed, Murdered, Mail Delivery to Chicago Suspended

Piracy: Vista Ferry, Attacked, Robbed, Dozens of Passengers and Crew Casualties

Six Killed, 12 Wounded in Party Drive by Shooting, No Arrests

Lake Marina Invaded, Robbed, Dozens of Boats Damaged, Hundreds Injured

Car Dealership Raided, 56 Cars Stolen, 14 Staff Murdered

Three Killed, Two Children Under Five Years Old Wounded, in Gang Crossfire. Charges Dropped for Insufficient Evidence

Woman Thrown From Overhead Train by Homeless Man With 34 Pending Criminal Charges, Free Without Bond

Busy Restaurant Invasion, Robbery, Many Killed and Injured

99th Smash and Grab Jewelry Robbery Leads to Death of Store Owner, Three Others, No Arrests

989 Violent Felons Released Early From Illinois Prisons on Clemency by Governor

State Attorney General Will Not Prosecute Minors Guilty of Armed Robbery, Rape, Carjacking, Burglary, Instead Divert to Counseling

State Attorney General Will Not Seek Death Penalty in Any Case, Death Row Closed

District Attorneys Will Not Prosecute Trespassing, Petty Theft, Shop Lifting, Simple Assault, or Armed Robbery if Gun is Not Used as These Crimes Involve Property and or Damages That are Covered by Insurance

Mass Resignations of Police at CPD in Protest

16 People Including Mother and Child Die of Drug Overdose in Local Park

Woman Killed, 14-Year-Old Daughter Raped by Three Men in 243rd Home Invasion of the Year, No Arrests Charges Reduced by Prosecutor to Manslaughter in Killing of Three Sisters, Plea Deal Results in 30 Months in Prison, Suspended, Probation Given

Federal Attorney Refuses to Prosecute BLMN for Burning Down Courthouse, Saying it Was Done at Night and Was an Accident, All 11 Freed

No Pre-Trial Incarceration in Criminal Cases, No Matter Criminal Past or Danger to Society, Governor Says Innocent Until Proven Guilty

Mayor Heavyhand Calls Skyrocketing Crime Report Fake News

Recidivist Pedophile Released Over Objection of Child Victim's Mother, Child Found Molested and Murdered, Pedophile Re-Arrested, Released

Justice of Appellant Court Now on Supreme Court Rules Consumption of Child Porn is Different Than Distribution, Frees 58 Pedophiles, Apologizes to Them for Any Inconvenience

Fishing Boats, Captured, Burned, Many Casualties

Six Parents Arrested at School Board Meeting by FBI for Violating Ban on Public Speaking About CRTE Man Robs Dozens of Items From Local CVS, No Charges, DA Says He Was Only Stealing Food, Clothing, Medicine Necessities, It's OK

Wounded Veteran With One Remaining Limb

Dragged From Home by 32 FBI Agents for Attending Outside Capital Demonstration Against Election, No Release, Bond Set at $1,000,000.00, Denied Medical Care in Custody

Two-Time Beauty Queen and Law Student Falls From 29th Floor Balcony, Boyfriend Says She Jumped Because She Thought She Could Fly

Illegal Alien Uses Machete to Slice and Dice Female Victim, Takes $20.00 and Her Cell Phone

Accused Shooter in Three Other Crimes Free Without Bond Kills Girlfriend and Daughter, Claims Self-Defense, Bond Set at $5,000.00

66 Drive By Shootings in One Day Sets Record in Chicago, 96 People Wounded, No Arrests

Two State Troopers Run Over and Killed With a Third Man by Anti-Police Woman and Thug Boyfriend

24 Arson Fires Burn in the City, Entire Office Building and Security Consumed

Elderly Woman Pushed to Her Death on Subway Tracks as Dozens Watch in Horror, Leaves Scene on Train, Disappears

Elder Home Invaded, Residents All Robbed, Six Dead, 49 Wounded

Bisexual Transgender Transsexual Stabs Her Boyfriend for Lying About Her Sexual Preference for Group Sex, Released Without Bond, Asked to be Nice by District Attorney Office

Woman Carjacking Victim, Coat Stuck in Door, Dragged Four Miles to Her Death by Three Gang Members Out on Own Recognizance for 11 Robbery Charges, All Illegal Aliens Previously Deported

Victim, Sergio Sanchez, Robbed of His Shoes by Cutting Off Both Feet by Drugged-Up Assailant, Found Dead in Trunk of Car, Killer Referred to Psychiatric Care, Mother Claims Racism as a Defense, it Made Him Crazy, He Needed New Shoes

Female Internet influencer, 14 Years of Age, Pushed From Roof Top by Unidentified Man, Found Dead on Sidewalk

76 BLMN Members Occupy 16 Family Homes Around the City, Refuse to Leave, Saying, "This is Our Land, You Stole, We Want Equity," and Authorities Refuse to Intervene, It's a Civil Matter

Cannibalism Suspected in Eating of Hearts of Three Tortured Victims in Rear of MS16 Gang Headquarters, MS 16 Knows Nothing

Police Substation Attacked, Burned, Many Injuries, No Arrests

More on TV with better pictures. No one understood, at least that is how it seemed, anyway. Victims' families can make claims for redress. Money the measure of all things.

Crime was getting WORSE.

Chapter 20

Friday night all went to the Mosque, to be with the faithful, in the house of Allah. It was a relief, to say the least, for the families, men, women and children.

Nothing like communal prayers, worship, and a small inspiring sermon on the grace and mercy of Allah. There was tea, cakes and comradery.

Aslan, Tamara and Yasmine all joined the women's group. They talked up a storm, shared cell numbers, and made new friends. Rashid and Ramin joined the men's club. Hamid would be filled in later.

Overall, it was a blessing, like being home again.

It was past 10:00 p.m. When Faisil and Farhad signaled it was time to depart.

Ramin noticed, "We are all ready. Thank you for the beautiful evening. I will collect the others and meet you out front in two minutes."

Travel home to the HCA was a short distance, but still there was time for conversation. Aslan spoke first.

"Faisil, thank you. It is wonderful to know all our brothers and sisters and Fatima. She is so nice. I must express myself – it is so different, the peace and love inside the Mosque compared to the crime and violence outside."

Faisil answered, "I agree, and Abdul, he is so nice too. Sad the USA is so behind in comparison to the rest of the world. They just don't know it yet. That fellow, Trump, trying to Make

America Great, was the last strong voice."

"What do you mean behind?"

"The majority of people are good but have no control. Censorship blocks knowledge and they can only think and talk the lies the media and tech tell them. There is no debate. Only communist messaging in schools, on TV, and by tech. There is no free speech and plenty of crime."

Aslan heard every word, "This is like the Taliban, but worse."

"Worse. If the truth does get out, media and tech name call, attack and cancel and destroy the person. They call it Russian disinformation. Like Gunter Brandon's laptop, the FBI says it is disinformation to protect the regime. Everyone knows it is real."

"Funny, the whole idea of global warming, the war on U.S. energy and oil, to shut it down, as President Brandon and the leftists want, the critical race theory, and teaching racism and division. All this propaganda about transsexuals – this is Russian and Chinese disinformation, calculated to hurt the U.S. It is hurting, and no one knows. No one dares to say it."

"There must be a reason for this. It must be helping the country, no?"

"The lack of truth destroys election integrity, corrupts at all levels, destroys free speech, equal justice, and due process. No one is treated fairly unless he is part of the D.C. cabal. Crime against property and persons is promoted in the name of social justice. Borders are open to drugs, criminals and millions of illegal aliens. None of whom want to work now that they get tax refunds for not paying tax. All of whom want welfare, housing and healthcare, all kept secret, as the nation sinks and the poor taxpayers go broke under heavy taxes, inflation, and a lack of opportunity."

"What about education? That is opportunity, no?"

"Yes, but teachers union, socialists, teaching anti-racism that is actually racism. Giving hormones to children to change sex, often leading to depression and suicide. Children learn nothing and no one cares. Fully 63% of children drop out of school here. Imagine that in the age of knowledge, whereas in Korea, Japan, China, India, my beloved Pakistan, where children jump off buildings if they fail a test. They want knowledge and to get ahead. Here, children want to flunk out of school and flunk into a gang and have illegitimate children with women they never see again. This creates opportunity for us. We have no competition from citizens or illegals, we swim, they sink."

"Is that why my dear Faisil, you have a new, big, beautiful truck?"

"Yip, and I paid $62,000.00 cash. Thanks to God, it is mine and not the bank's."

"Time to say thank you and good night. There is the HCA. Very informative," said Rashid, "OK everyone, let's get some sleep, if you can after listening to Faisil. Oh my."

Chapter 21

As it turned out, Ramin worked the whole weekend. Hamid too, but only in the afternoons until 10:00 p.m. He and Rashid accompanied the women and children back to the Mosque for Saturday teachings and socializing.

A full day, satisfying and rewarding.

Aslan, Tamara and Yasmine, enjoyed their friends, especially Abdul and Fatima, 2nd generation immigrants. They were both in their twenties, and it seemed Fatima was sweet on Abdul. The women could not wait to come back next weekend, God willing.

Local news was always on the TV during dinner hour which was now held in Tamara's apartment. Aslan teased Rashid about gaining some weight. "No," he said, "I just regained what I have lost. It's OK."

"Yes, darling, it is fine."

A scream from Tamara caught everyone's attention. "Oh my God," she said, pointing at the TV.

The news person was just saying, "I am reporting live from the LaQuinta Downtown where there has been another smash and grab robbery in the on-property jewelry store. The 146th such brazen robbery this year. This one, with a tragic result, as an employee of the hotel of which we only have his first name as Reuben, a Food Manager, tried to intervene and was hit several times with a hammer. He was pronounced dead at the scene. There are no suspects at this time. Bobby Rose reporting for WRXY TV."

The three children broke down in tears. They loved Reuben. The adults silently stared at each other. No one knew what to say. No one was happy with the news and no one was going to forget it.

The next day while on patrol, Ramin took flowers and an envelope with money to the LaQuinta for Reuben's family, with a sympathy note. He had told the others of his intent. He figured that was all that could be done for now.

He asked Maria, "Do you know who these criminals are?"

"No senor, no one knows or much cares."

"I care, Maria."

When Ramin got home, things were more upbeat.

Rashid was proudly holding up a copy of the city page of the Tribunal about his first story, the "Lamb Shanks and Ethnic Cuisine 2022." Rashid announced his next story was on Mexican Korean Fusion and he would go with his editor tomorrow for a taste. This was Rashid in full color. He had brought a happy moment and relief from the distress they all felt.

When Ramin complimented him, it was obvious Rashid really needed the stroke.

In Rashid's reality, it was Ramin that had best friends – warrior brothers. He was their best friend and the bonds were clear and forever.

On the other hand, Rashid had many friends. Some he thought of as his best friends. Some were simply what the Chinese call Chop Friends, meaning someone to have lunch with but not to be trusted. Rashid always knew that none of his best friends considered him to be their best friend – they all had other, better friends. In Ramin he had a big brother, a warrior, and a mutual, trusted and loved best friend forever.

Usually tight lipped, Ramin talked as well. He told the group about going to the LaQuinta and about how he now knew so much about the city, the streets, and people. He said, "You know, I now have so many coworkers. I ride with different ones and they are all so disgusted with the Democrats. They say in two years they will have destroyed the future of the people."

"Surprising," he said, "coming from so many working people."

Rashid replied, "I can see at the Tribunal, they are woke. This means young, arrogant and stupid to me. Most have never traveled, can't speak other languages, know nothing about the real world, and are very nasty to others. Sorry, my dear brother, even the Army is woke. No wonder the Taliban won the war."

"What do you do?"

"I say nothing, just do my job."

Hamid wondered aloud, "So where is the justice. We have no sharia here?"

Ramin had read some old captured Russian papers quoting Mao Tse Tung, "The only justice in the world comes out of a barrel of a gun."

That summed it up for Ramin. No fear.

Chapter 22

Ramin had almost forgotten it was Jamil's birthday. He knew his wife could not get out and no celebration was planned. So he asked his coworker on patrol, where to get a cake. Of course, he knew.

Ramin purchased a nice Superman Cake for $56.00. To him, this was costly, but his son deserved to feel special, at least for this day. Superman would do fine.

Dinner had moved to Yasmine's apartment by now, so Ramin dropped the cake off with her after work. Before dinner, there were prayers and the usual community meal. No one said anything about the birthday. Ramin asked the adults to say nothing, to keep it a surprise. He liked surprises, like surprise ambushes from his old war days. When Yasmine brought out the cake, milk and tea, the cheers abounded.

"Happy Birthday, Jamil and Many More, inish Allah."

Tamara knew how to approach the cake cutting. She knew children wanted fairness, equal treatment – nothing more or less. So she had a rule that Jamil cuts and Mona picks.

The pieces were exact in size, like precise measurements. It always made her laugh. She knew everyone wanted equal treatment and deserved it.

The cake was not too sweet, actually delicious, and there was not a piece left to share with his coworker. Ramin would have to explain, "Sorry, none for you my friend. It's all gone."

Later, Yasmine confided in Ramin. He was someone she always leaned on. She asked him to please arrange for her to see a doctor. She was not sure how to do it. She wanted to get there without Hamid knowing.

"Ramin, dear brother, I believe I am with child. But I do not want to say anything until I am certain. I do not want Hamid to get his hopes up falsely after what we have endured, you know."

"Inish Allah, I hope for good news. I will arrange everything. Give me your medical card. At the right moment, I will pick you up with our patrol car and run you to the doctor. Call us when you're done and we will run you home. No problem. I will let you know early tomorrow."

"Thank you, Ramin."

Ramin was excited for Hamid. He had never recovered from the loss of his child back home. He hoped this would work out for him. He had his fingers crossed. This was good news for a change. A birthday celebration and the coming, perhaps, of a new child.

Luck was with them. The appointment was set for the next Friday, at 10:00 a.m. Hamid was off that day and the children were in school. Ramin called to pick up Yasmine. "Just tell Hamid I need you to shop for a gift for Tamara and you will be back in an hour."

It turned out to be two hours, but Yasmine was still back in plenty of time to pick up the children. She had good news to share with Hamid when it was the right time. She was thankful, excited and wanted to share, but needed more time to mature. When she told Ramin, they hugged, and she asked him to remain silent for a few more days.

"No problem, do as you need. I am here for you." He smiled broadly.

She laughed, "Ramin, look at you, thank you, brother."

After prayers, everyone was ready for the services at the Mosque. Faisil and Farhad picked everyone up right on time and arrived early, only to confusion.

People were standing in groups, outside and inside, speaking different languages and dialects. But it was clear something was dreadfully wrong.

Farhad asked everyone to wait by the trucks and ran in. He soon came out with the bad news. Young Abdul returned with him. They were in anguish.

Farhad looked at Ramin, with great pain in his voice, announced to the nervous gathering that Fatima had been a victim of hit and run, and was dead. This hit the women of the group very hard. The girls all covered their faces and cried.

Yasmine and Aslan tried to hold up. Tamara simply fainted, caught at the last second by Rashid. There was no way to console anyone.

Ramin was steady, "Rest her soul, poor little girl. Do they know any facts?"

Farhad replied, "Yes, brother, witnesses told the police that a man on the passenger side of the car yelled at her, go home towel head."

Ramin had heard that before. "Do you know if the car was yellow?"

"Yes, yellow, how did you guess?"

"Not guess, I know. We shall not forgive. We will make this right."

Ramin was filled with rage. He knew what to do.

Ramin could see young Abdul was destroyed. No one ever thinks about victims, family or loved ones. Ramin knew. He reached over and put Abdul in a bear hug that was so strong that Abdul felt strength. It buoyed him up to face the reality.

"Abdul, I know you live alone. You will come and live with Hamid in the near future. You are now part of our family. I will not accept a no."

"Thank you Ramin. Is it OK, Hamid?"

Yasmine answered, "It is done, you will join us."

Over the PA, Imam Akeem asked everyone to come into the Mosque for prayers. He would make an announcement.

There was a calm silence as everyone filed in. Imam lead prayer.

The Imam dispatched two men and two women to the morgue to retrieve Fatima for washing of the body, burial shroud, and for burial tomorrow in the Moslem section of the cemetery. In Islam there were rules and timelines. There would be no delay.

He said there would be tea and sweets served at the Mosque after the burial for anyone wishing to pay respect to Fatima's small family and friends.

With Abdul in hand, the group was driven first to his place to pick up some things, then to the HCA. It was an early night for everyone. Sleep helped heal the pain.

Faisil would pick Abdul up the next day for the events to follow. The other men had to work and Ramin told the women and children to stay home. He wanted them safe at home.

On Saturday, as the men were heading for the bus, Diana approached them. It was her day off when she had heard the news. She expressed her sorrow and told them she would visit the ladies for the day. She had cancelled a visit with her mother.

Rashid was moved by this. He could notice and could feel her sincerity.

The men all nodded and thanked her, "God blessings unto you. We must go now."

"Thank you."

Chapter 23

The next week was all about the children and the Easter Holiday, coming soon, and the Easter Egg Hunt at school. No one knew just how rabbits laid eggs. None of the kids cared. It was all about chocolate eggs, drawings and pastels, and dying eggs at home the evening before the big hunt which was set for Friday.

The women all enjoyed the festivities, along with the children. It was a party. The men did not get it but they went along anyway. Why not, this is fun, it is religious, and teaches goodness and brotherly love.

Thursday evening was an experience for everyone. There were boiled eggs, chocolate eggs – small ones, and lots and lots of pots full of color to dye them in so many imaginative ways. It was obvious that Magi and Mona were both very artistic and you could hear Aslan telling them many times, "Oh my, that is so pretty. How did you get all those colors on the eggs? So amazing."

It was fun.

Because Ramin was out and about the city in the patrol car most of the day, he was elected to get some chocolate eggs for everyone. The ones with all the pretty flowers, chocolate filled, vanilla filled, and, of course, maple nut filled. It cost him over $94.00 and he laughed out loud at enormous amount of chocolate yet appreciated the beauty of the Bitmans Chocolate products and the fancy boxes.

He also found a favorite of his own, the dark chocolate Bordeaux. He had several small pieces and could not wait to share. He felt like a child, again.

Needless to say, the small Bordeaux pieces were a hit at home, and Ramin insisted the others open their own egg treats on Friday to enjoy on the weekend. This was all new to everyone. The delay only created more excitement. Everyone loves Easter.

On Friday, everyone lined the school yard perimeter, standing and waiting for the Easter Egg Hunt to begin. It was great to see 300 children of all shapes, sizes and backgrounds pour out of the classrooms and onto the grass to find glory. It happened with lots of pictures and screams of happiness. How fun it was for everyone.

Every child seemed to find something including Jamil, Amy, Mona and Magi. Not the expensive sort Ramin bought but so good. Prizes were awarded to so many happy children. Smiles everywhere. This was a beautiful moment for all, so beautiful.

Home at last and tired, the eggs Ramin had purchased, every one was opened and sampled. Every one of them.

"Mommy, I really like this one. What is it? It has nuts in it," said Jamil.

"Me too," echoed Magi.

Not Mona, she dug the maple nut filling with flowers, "I really like this one, I don't want it to end."

Tamara replied, "Enough, enough, save the rest. We have the whole weekend, and we must pray and have some food. Then we go to Mosque."

So, it was.

This may have been the happiest day these new immigrants had enjoyed in Chicago. The men were all grateful to Allah for the pleasant times.

Even better, Yasmine told Hamid she was with child, a girl. Hamid was ecstatic. God willing, they would have the chance, one day soon, to name the newborn.

Hamid said what they both were thinking, "We shall call her Aslan, inish Allah."

Chapter 24

Mid week, just before dinner, Aslan announced, "Oh no, we are out of Labneh and we need it for dinner." Lebneh, the famous yogurt cheese, is great with olive oil, olives, vegetables, and so many things.

Ramin said he would run across to the International Market and pick some up along with a piece of Tuma cheese.

A good idea goes bad.

Just outside the store, his panic button went off. At once he drew his new Lima Full Tang hunting knife from its sheath. Sure enough, out ran a man in a black hoodie, small caliber automatic still in his right hand, pointed right at Ramin's head.

Before the robber could shoot, Ramin pushed his firing arm to the right, spun him around against the wall, stuck him in the left kidney, as he was trained. There was no sound out of the bad guy's mouth, just like it is supposed to go down. He stuck him again, as was his practice. Like the Garfeld cartoon he had seen as a kid, spiders and bad things play dead, better to kill them twice. This little comic rule had saved Ramin a couple times in his past and he remembered it.

He could now hear, fixed on the scream of Khalil, "Noor, are you OK? Please help, oh my God," as he held her off the floor in his arms.

Ramin called 911 with one finger on the emergency button and got help. He put an arm around Khalil and moved him away. He could see she was hit in the lower left abdomen – nothing so important there, and told Khalil, "Just relax, she will be fine. Put some firm pressure here," placing Khalil's hand over the wound.

The CPD arrived with fire and ambulance just as Diana walked through the door. It was the same Sergeant on the scene that met Ramin in the park. Diana told him Ramin was golden and asked how the bad guy was?

"Bad guy not good, crime scene is on the way for his body."

"Your friend, Ramin, is a tough fellow. I've seen him before, he works in security."

"Yes, he is my Afghan Special Ops Captain and neighbor. Take him outside and get his statement. I will wait here with the other Officer and Khalil. Just get the EMTs in ASAP."

Ramin gave his statement. His knife was legal carry. EMTs took both Khalil and Noor to the ER. She would be fine. Ramin picked up and paid for the Labneh and forgot his favorite Tuma.

After the scene was secured, Diana would drop by to check on everyone.

By the time Ramin got home, dinner was done and the children were in bed. He had to clean up in time for Diana's knock on the door. The adults sat together. Diana had an Amstall beer she took and paid for from the market and she wondered aloud, "Is this what you have to do to buy cheese?"

Ramin, unflappable, answered, "Seems so, at least for now."

The market was closed for four days. Before long, Khalil was back and the store was open for business. Ramin told Khalil to get a .38 Special revolver for under the counter. "It's a six shot, but load five. If you use it, shoot them all."

Abdul, still suffering himself, was already in the store helping Khalil. "Ramin, this is so terrible. Seems impossible to make right."

Ramin, not a scholar, had heard his brother. He repeated,

"Napoleon said impossible is impossible. In the eyes of Allah, nothing is impossible. Have no fear."

Khalil thanked him for everything. "Thank you, too, for saving my wife." Khalil marveled at the man Allah had made in Ramin. He was a rock.

He had a feeling something was cooking within this man.

Chapter 25

The next few days of spring were better with the sun up, cool breezes, and Chicago food to sample, as seen on local TV.

For some reason Ramin got May Day off.

Aslan had seen the Bavarian Cream Filled Super Donut from Randi Donuts and wanted, so badly, to try them.

It's a done deal. Ramin went to get a Vietnamese dozen, which is 14 with two free ones. It was an afternoon snack for Aslan and the others.

Even Hamid was still home to enjoy them.

"Oh my, these are so far out good," said Yasmine, "I could eat two."

Ramin knew she was eating for two anyway and said, "Please do."

"Save one for Diana. You know the police love donuts," Rashid said.

Everyone agreed. Coffee followed this time, and it was perfect.

That very afternoon Diana called, "Don't cook. I will bring real Chicago Pizza with no pork or lard. You will love it. And if OK, I will bring a beer for me."

At 5:30 p.m. sharp, she pulled into the parking lot. Yasmine and Tamara helped her up. There is nothing like real Chicago Pizza.

Diana ate three pieces. She also got her donut.

"Next time we will have real Kosher Chicago Dogs. People live here just for those babies," Diana said.

No argument from anyone. Maybe on the weekend. Ramin knew because he had one with his partner a few days ago. He smiled and said, "With some chips too."

Prayers, baths, and sleep early for another day is coming. God willing another good one.

Chapter 26

Sadly, not to be.

After school...

"Hey, little girl, want to get high? Oh yeah," the creepy man said to Magi in the park on an otherwise beautiful spring day. Aslan pulled the little girl away and pushed the man down.

He came up in an instant and stabbed her in the stomach. Aslan froze. She knew she was hurt. Both children hugged her tight, staining their little faces with their mother's blood. Blood that had given them life. Aslan fell on top of them, never to move again.

Aslan's suffering was over. Her soul now in Heaven, to be with Allah. A lifetime of victim suffering for the little girls and the family had just begun because of one evil predator allowed to roam free.

How can one person, any person, cause such suffering, do such lasting harm, in a civilized society? This was not his first murder, but it would be his last.

The event quickly shook the surroundings. A news helicopter appeared overhead. There was live streaming on TV, police scanners, EMT scanners, and news wires all lit up. Aslan's loved ones knew and headed straight to Elgin Park.

A soccer coach and his wife were already on scene. He tried to help Aslan but could do nothing more than hold her while his wife cradled the crying children.

CPD arrived along with the Sergeant and several squad cars.

He already had the killer face down, cuffed and murder weapon recovered.

Ramin was first to arrive from afar and checked Aslan's pulse just as paramedics poured over her. There was nothing. He ran over to the captive, "I want to see his face."

The Sergeant rolled over the creep and Ramin got to see his face before the police dragged the killer away.

Rashid went with Aslan in the ambulance. To where, Ramin didn't know. He got the clan home to his apartment only to find Farhad and Faisil already there with Abdul. There was silent shock, except for the whimpering of Jamil and the girls. Grief everlasting.

Sitting together like lifeless figures themselves, no one moved until Diana knocked on the door. Ramin opened it.

"Hello Ramin. I am so sorry, so sorry, deja vu. I hope you will all be OK."

"Thank you, we await Rashid's return. I cannot leave the family."

"Of course, Ramin. I am going downtown. I will get Aslan's body released and to the cemetery by noon tomorrow. Please call the Imam to be there with his team to prepare for burial in the afternoon, as is your custom. Don't let Rashid out of your sight, I worry about him. OK?"

"Thank you. Consider it done."

Faisil heard every word.

"Ramin, do not fret. I go now to the Mosque and arrange everything. Do not worry about details or money. We shall cover it all. I will go now. See you soon."

He followed Diana out the door.

Ramin was now in combat mode. Injured but working on achieving objectives, something therapeutic for the man. He fixed small snacks and tea for everyone, even the ladies, so everyone could have sustenance and rest until tomorrow.

Later in the evening, Farhad brought Rashid into the apartment. Ramin hadn't noticed that Farhad had left. Ramin pulled Rashid to him, hugged him like he had never hugged any person in his life before and did not let him go. With nothing said they sat together, Rashid's head on Ramin's shoulder for the rest of the night.

Everyone slept in place, except Ramin. He was up all night, eyes open, in a sort of dreamscape swirling around and within him. Perhaps a vision, a calling, a direction. He was not sure what it was, but he got the message. It was time to take charge of the battlefield.

Everyone was present at the cemetery by 1:00 p.m. The grave side service was performed by Imam Akeem. Diana was close by with her hair covered and her sunglasses concealed her tears.

Aslan was laid to rest forever. Ramin never left Rashid's side as he had promised Diana.

There was no follow up meal and no socializing at the Mosque. Not this time. Spent time at home to sit, drink some tea, give strength to the children, and have faith that Aslan was with Allah.

Three women from the Mosque stayed on to give their support to the family.

Diana made the point to Rashid that she would come over to visit the children every day – to give them some sort of grounding in this new world and to show them some love.

Rashid thanked her for this and invited her to dine with the family, as family. This sounded pretty good to her and she could comfort the family and learn their ways.

By 8:00 p.m. the family was asleep, including Rashid, who was exhausted.

Mrs. Jinx left a tuna casserole in the apartment for them before they got home, for dinner tomorrow.

Around 9:00 p.m. Diana came to see Ramin and she had a steely look in her blue eyes.

Ramin welcomed her in. She asked for him to step out for a second and he did.

"At least the criminal is behind bars and he should hang," said Ramin.

"Not quite. The killer, with 17 prior arrests and some for violence, was out on his own recognizance for two separate felony arrests. He was awaiting trials and out on bond for an arrest in Indiana. He had two probation violations."

"The jail will release him tonight at midnight with his knife. It was a legal weapon."

"Why would anyone release this person?"

"You know, Ramin, innocent until proven guilty. No pre-trial incarceration, they just go free and repeat the same crimes on the innocent. That is police work today."

"Prosecutors don't prosecute. Judges don't uphold the law. People say Hors Goros, billionaires, who want a world government, see the U.S.A. as an obstacle, want to tear it down, so they are behind fake elections, fake news, hate speech, division, chaos, and fear, and high crime, caused by their bought-and- owned, socialist, soft-on-crime prosecutors. It seems to be working."

Their eyes locked. Ramin really admired Diana very much. He knew why she had told him. He knew, she knew, he knew how to kill this murderer.

At 12:06 a.m., behind the central jail, with not a word said, Ramin did – he killed him twice as was his custom.

The Tribunal Newspaper picked up the story, it seemed headless corpses made the news even in Chicago.

It had begun, the cleaning of the devil from Chicago forever.

There was no work for anyone for a week. They received paid family leave which was a blessing for everyone.

Chapter 27

The next day, Faisil picked up Ramin and Rashid. Imam Akeem wanted to see them both, now, at the Mosque.

Imam Akeem himself was a veteran of the Army and he had had enough.

The community needed the help of God and the guidance of Imam Ali, the blind Imam in Indiana who is the son of Mulla Ali at the famous Mulla Ali Mosque. He must be consulted for divine guidance.

Imam Akeem did not listen but only spoke. "Tomorrow, you will leave by 10:00 a.m., inish Allah, to visit our dear brother Imam Ali. Faisil knows the way. It has been arranged. They await your safe arrival. Report back to me once you return."

"God's blessings upon all of you."

Both Tamara and Yasmine waited for the men to return from the Mosque. When the men arrived, saw the women, they knew at once what was to come.

Tamara and Yasmine sat at the dining room table. Yasmine was already smoking, even though she had stopped two months ago. Tamara was lighting a Camel, the match shook in her hand.

The women's eyes through the smoke could be seen to glow red with rage. Tamara spoke first.

"Sit down, we shall talk now." The men sat down, not a word said.

Yasmine told them that Tamara would speak for both of them.

She did, exactly as the men expected.

"We are your family, Aslan is your family, we follow you, even to this new country, we have your children, we raise them in the manner you desire, we cook for the family, clean. Support you in all things. We cover our skin, and hair, we are modest and humble, and we respect you and revere Allah."

"We are all suffering, the children too, you are the men, our men, what are you going to do to make this right, for all of us?"

"Do not think even for a second we accept this, that tomorrow will be like before, it will not be, we want you to be men, to do your duty, to make this right."

"I know you understand your duty."

The men well knew the duty, the women had laid down the law, they would never accept them or anything unless and until their men put matters right, no matter the costs, no matter the risks. It must be done, or there would never again be a normal day.

Ramin answered for the men, he knew there was but one thing these women would accept, "We shall do our duty, we shall make it right, God willing, you will be satisfied, we swear."

The next morning, after an early, 6-hour drive, the F150 King Cab pulled into the parking lot of Mulla Ali Mosque – a beautiful Mosque in Indiana. Faisil announced, "Welcome to Mulla Ali Mosque. Imam Ali's late father founded it decades ago. There have been Moslems in America for centuries. This Imam, as you already know, is blind, reads to Koran in braille, but he is said to have memorized it all. I believe it."

Ramin riding shotgun heard every word. "Indeed, thank you, Faisil. This place is rich in splendor and very big. I am impressed and hoping we find support as well."

Morning prayers had just begun, so the members of the group

all joined in. This was one of the first prayers in a Mosque in America, with brothers and sisters in Islam and an Imam. It was joyous and spiritually rewarding and gratifying occasion for everyone. Tea followed and then the meeting began.

In the Salon, at the side of the great hall, sat about 40 men. Their backs against the four walls, sitting on beautiful Persian carpets with Imam Ali, himself setting against the far wall opposite the entry door where the travelers stood.

"A salaam amalecum," the Imam called out. "Welcome. Come in. Please sit with us."

"Malecum salaam, a salaam amalecum," was the universal reply, with hands over their hearts. Ramin lead the way to a space on the rear wall followed by Rashid, Faisil and Hamid. They sat down to join the group.

The Imam began, "Welcome Moslem brothers. We feel joy and wish you all the grace that Allah may provide to the devout. As you can see, our congregation is large, thanks to God. It is made up of brothers and sisters from around the globe."

Waiving his hand so as to point, "We have so many, Pakistanis, Afghanis, Uzbeks, Turkmenians, Chenchens, yes, Uygurs, Indians, Iranians and, of course, our brothers and sisters that are Turks, Syrians, Egyptians, Jordanians, Arabs, Iraqis, Somalis, Africans, many Sudanese, even Chinese, some Russian brothers – American brothers and sisters too. We love this great nation of America, our home, as Allah has dictated."

"Imam Cemal, please moderate the meeting."

Imam Cemal sat to the right of Imam Ali. "Welcome one and all. The first order of business is to introduce our newest converts, Americans, who have heard the word of Allah and have a new religion and names too. Please stand," pointing to a group of three couples, "Imam Karimov, is pleased to introduce."

"Thank you, Imam Ali," said Imam Cemal, "yes, this is Yousef and his wife, Afina, and Nabil and his wife Fayruz, and Bilal and his wife Alea, our newest brothers and sisters in Islam."

Everyone in the room wore masks and the young women covered their hair. Yousef wore the uniform of the United States Army. He was a sergeant, and he, like the other men wore a beard. Yousef and Afina were proud African Americans as well.

Imam Ali warmly welcomed them, saying, "Islam does not have missionaries. Nor does Islam ask anyone, no less force anyone, to be a Moslem. But Islam is a religion that welcomes all, so Allah's blessings upon you."

The new members all nodded their heads in thanks.

"I understand you read the Holy Koran in English. Who among you will remind our brothers and sisters of the Pillars of Islam?"

Before anyone could reply, sister Afina spoke. "Imams, brothers and sisters, there is but one God, the Almighty, Merciful Allah. Mohammad, praise be unto him, is his worthy Prophet, that during life, if a believer can, he or she should make a pilgrimage to Mecca."

"Allah Akbar," was heard around the room.

Imam Ali thanked Afina. "Slightly abbreviated but very well said, the pillars are simple and important, as each believer must keep his or her faith. In Islam, there is no middle man between a Moslem and Allah. There is no alter, no front or back of the Mosque. Many are round with no pews. We are all brothers and sisters and equals together before Allah."

"Please join us for worship. You are most welcome. Bring your children too, when you are blessed with them."

With that Imam Karmmov and the newly devout took their leave of the meeting with the usual bows and farewells. It took about three minutes. Hamid made the obvious comment, "In Islam, it takes longer to say hello and goodbye than to hold the whole meeting."

So True.

It was back to Imam Cemal. "The next order of business is charity. As you know, there are over 100,000 Moslem doctors in the United States. For the many famous surgeons that save lives every day, may Allah's blessings be upon them. Several work at St. Jude Hospital for children and the Shriner's Hospital for children. They have told us and we believe they are fine charity hospitals, doing the work of Allah. We make charitable contributions not only abroad but here too. So, Imam Babu, please make your report."

"Thank you, my brother. I am happy to report our Eid collection for the two charities alone raised over $100,000.00. The Mosque shall happily bestow on each of them $50,000.00. This is being done with God's grace and direction, to help do the work of Allah for the poor, the sick, and the disabled, in a caring and loving manner. God's blessing to all."

Imam Ali, visibly grateful, said, "Wonderful work in the name of Allah. My brother Imam Babu, in a way I wish our new members were here now. It would be good to let them see that Islam is a religion of peace, of love, of compassion, of charity and not just within the Moslem community but within the community of all man. No matter of race, creed, color, and religion. We accept all religions and believers, even outside of Islam, as we know their hearts are pure."

"Even in Jerusalem, Islam has always guarded the holy places of every other religion. It is my hope that they will see this divine path for themselves, and, of course, they feel as we all do that Jerusalem has always been and is, and share forever be, a Moslem city, sharing it with all our other brothers and sisters of various religions."

Imam Cemal said, "The final business concerns our guests from Chicago. Thank you for coming and God's blessings upon all of you. We understand from the news sent to us by our friend, honorable Faisil, who has been so generous to our Mosque, that you are troubled with the situation in Chicago. We are deeply aware, and we extend our condolences to you for

147

your losses. We have about 50 Mosques and Moslem groups in that city, and they report as well. Indeed, there are representatives from 18 Chicago Mosques with us today," pointing to the men sitting just to his right, "we have heard their many stories. Please tell us your story. Who is your spokesman?"

"Dear Brothers, it shall be Rashid. Rashid, you have the honor, please," announced Faisil.

Rashid spoke mostly in English, but he dipped into at least four other languages to make his points. Everyone listened to every word. Many shook their heads in agreement. Some could be heard saying to themselves "How awful, unbelievable, disgusting."

Rashid talked for nearly one hour and he showed several news articles and pictures to help make his point. The point being that life in Chicago was unlivable, that the forces of the devil had taken over and it was getting worse and worse every day. There would be no safety for anyone and no future for the children. The Shytan was in control.

Even with all of this, the Imam insisted to know more. "Please do not stop and tell us more." And, he did. There was no doubt the Imam was shocked to the core.

The room began to buzz with conversations on all sides, in various dialects, loud voices, animated gestures, and organized chaos.

The Imam seemed to be concentrating. Trying to focus or hear something.

Then, the Imam was helped to stand upright, reaching above his head, looking up, he proclaimed, "There is no choice. Allah commands it. It is Jihad, Chicago Jihad, starting now."

Everyone was now on their feet, there could be no dissent, it was unanimous, the entire building seemed to tremble as the words reverberated through the structure.

"Allah Akbar, Allah Akbar." The Shytan, the devil, the evil of Chicago was about to meet its end.

The Imam, still on his feet, proclaimed to all present and to the Heavens above, "I summon to holy Jihad all Mujahadeen, as many as can free themselves for this divine duty, to come unto Chicago, to our Mosques, where they each shall be given shelter in the homes of our suffering brothers and sisters. 5,000 to 10,000 Mujahadeen, if they have arms, bring them too."

"I also call upon this gathering to put hands over hearts to work, not as many, but as one, and do all that is required to bring the equipment needed by the Mujahadeen to Chicago to cleanse the sinful and evil city. Do this today, now, before you leave."

"Talk of this only in person, face to face, and here at the Mosque. Use no artificial means of communication as we all know the tyrants of technology and ungodly people, who serve only the interests of the corrupt, the criminals, the perverts, the pornographers, the liars and fake news outlets, and themselves."

"It is still early so stay in this room and do everything in the name of Allah and the Prophet, praise be unto him, for Jihad, I have proclaimed."

"I must go now to pray. Allah Akbar."

The congregation now closed into a circle in the middle of the salon, everyone talking quietly, sharing ideas for discussion. Three water pipes were lit up. Some men smoked the fragrant charcoaled tobacco. Pots of tea and cups were brought in with some small graibi cookies.

Imam Cemal stayed to conduct the meeting. "The first thing is for the Chicago Mosques that are represented here, return to that City and notify all the other Mosques. Make them ready for the arrival of the Mujahadeen."

It was agreed. The 18 representatives would achieve this organization within the next five days, and everyone would return to this circle of brothers in two weeks to report. All the Mosques had much public space, halls, event centers, and many thousands of believers. This would be no problem.

Imam Cemal, himself and experience Mujahadeen, went on, "For the next four weeks, under the direction of brother Ramin, we will do recon, scoping out everything, all the evil places and evil doers in the city, so we know who the agents of shytan are. You will do this, Ramin?"

"I have already spoken to many brothers in arms from our past exploits. Yes, we shall organize and implement this and discover all we need to know and report back, God willing."

Imam Cemal was pleased.

"Faisil, thank you for your support. How long do you expect it to take to deliver our supplies for this divine and cleansing endeavor?"

"Four weeks from today."

"But I thought everything would come in from abroad, and the ports under this President Brandon were clogged up for months."

"This is true, Imam Cemal. They are clogged up because President Brandon and the Democrats imposed strict environmental rules so only new trucks, less than three years old, could call on a port to transport a container. Really stupid. Our shipment will come into Mazatlán, Mexico. It will then transit to Chicago avoiding all delays."

"Very well, we meet here again in two weeks for progress reports. We expect all hardware to be in Chicago in four weeks. We shall meet here in the 4th week for updates, planning and final delivery, God willing."

"Yes, Imam, give or take a few days for the final meeting. We shall be ready, inish Allah."

"Inish Allah."

"Please excuse me for 30 minutes. Talk among yourselves as I have a religious obligation to attend."

"Yes, Imam Cemal, we are talking. Thank you," answered Faisil.

For Ramin, this was a gratifying experience, brothers discussing what seemed like a military operation, all for Jihad. It was an obligation, an honor and he was excited.

The conversation, in various languages, buzzed around the circle of men at light speed. These men were all experienced warriors, some were trained by the Russians, others by the Americans, many by the Iranians, some by the Egyptians, and all with no fear. The Shytan, the devil, was in trouble.

Each man seemed to have his own favorite weapon. After a lengthy time of give and take, and no shortage of real war stories of valor, a list of essential equipment was completed. It included a pleasant variety. There was something for everyone which included:

- M 240B 7.26 mm Machine Gun, Quantity: 50

- M2A1 .50 cal. Heavy Machine Gun, Quantity: 6

- M430 300 mm Grenade Launcher-Heavy, Quantity: 1

- Claymore Mine, Command detonate, 680 grams C4, Quantity: 15

- M107 .50 Cal Sniper Rifle, Quantity: 3

- CAR -15 M4 Commando Carbine, 5.56 mm, Quantity: 350

- Barretta Model 92 FS, 9mm Semi Auto Ambi Pistol, Quantity: 350

- C4 Explosive, 150 Kilos

- RPG, 40 MM, Quantity: 100

- Lots of Ammo

Once all complied and printed off for all to see the smiles were everywhere among these warriors. For right, for good, for justice and they could not wait to get back into action.

Everyone was pumped. Let's go, man go.

Faisil took the list, asking, "Is this sufficient. The criminals have gone wild and are active 24/7?"

The answer came from Ramin. "If you can get more, fine. With this merchandise in our hands and with the help of Allah, a new day shall dawn in Chicago."

"You never know. I might be able to get a few Stinger missiles. You know the Ukrainians are corrupt and are now selling the missiles they got for free during the war."

"Everyone knows they are corrupt. They sold nukes to Iran and Syria in the 90's. This is no surprise, just dangerous to commercial airlines. It was crazy to send them those missiles."

"OK, so, maybe, we will get some Stingers too."

"Allah Akbar, Allah Akbar echoed through the hall with fists clinched and fire in the eye."

"You will bring us the Ahmad brothers, yes?"

"Yes."

Ramin reached over and shook Faisil's hand. "We are ready then."

By now, everyone was on their feet, hitting and hugging. Just then, Imam Ali came in and said, "I hear your voices. You are ready?"

A chorus answered, "Yes, Imam Ali, thank you. We are ready, God willing."

"So be it. Have a safe trip home. We will meet in 2 weeks, inish Allah, for follow up. You all understand. Good day."

Before leaving the Mosque, Rashid told Ramin he wanted to say goodbye to each person and use the bathroom before heading home.

"That is fine. We will wait for you at the truck."

While waiting for Rashid, Ramin asked, "OK, Faisil, how are we to pay for all of this military equipment, please?"

"You are from Afghanistan and you must ask me this. Really, my brother?"

"Well, yes."

"Here is your answer. I buy 1000 kilos of oven dried opium from your brothers and sisters back home. At the moment it is very cheap due to the situation – $200.00 a kilo. That is $200,000.00 and very cheap."

"Really?"

"Yes. We could buy morphine base, but I don't trust the Taliban chemists. You understand. So we go to the source, and it is not difficult to move the opium to Hong Kong or Thailand. We know and trust the labs there and in very short order they convert the opium into about 115 kilos of pure morphine base. They call it Pi Tzu. Did you know that?"

"We have heard."

"The Pi Tzu is in 1.3 kilo blocks, two inches by four inches by five inches. Small and easy to transport to Mexico where there are buyers paying for this size shipment, $5,000,000.00."

"The Mexicans convert it to about 125 kilos of heroin, worth about $8,000,000.00 in Mexico. Over $12,000,000.00 in the USA, where it is stepped on a few times, raising the market value to between $18,000,000.00 and $25,000,000.00."

"So, how do we pay?"

"We are done once the Pi Tzu lands in Mexico. We have nothing to do with the USA and we are paid in cash to be expecting $5,000,000.00. From that, we shall gladly pay $3,000,000.00 to the Taliban back home for the military hardware. They trust us for the money. We are repeat customers, leaving $2,000,000.00 gross over the $200,000.00 original investment. Less $250,000.00 for the cooks in Hong Kong or Thailand, leaving the net a little less than $2,000,000.00. All 90% of the hardware gets delivered."

"That does not seem to be enough money, no?"

"Why not? This President Brandon and the Democrats gave the Taliban over $86,000,000,000.00 of equipment for free. They don't worry at all about this size of business. It is nothing to them and they want the U.S. Dollars. Plus, the U.S. just gave the Taliban another $300,000,000.00 for bribe to be able to rescue the left behinds. The U.S. and U.N. just gave another $1,000,000,000.00 too. The Taliban is rich."

"Wow, so stupid, and the Mexicans, what about them?"

"They will take some of the equipment and we will look the other way. They will take 10% of it all. This cannot be helped. It is the cost of doing repeat business."

"But the hardware is in Mexico, not Chicago, what then?"

"That's easy. The Mexican cartels, now that they have the morphine base and have been paid, take care of it. Over the southern border is the first stop, usually to Kansas City. Then delivery in Chicago to the Mosques we already discussed, for temporary storage."

"Faisil, how can they cross the border? Don't the Americans have Border Guards? This does not seem possible, nowhere in the world, no way?"

"No way. Yes way, it is absolutely secure. The cartels control the entire southern border. They are moving over 6,000 people a day over the border. People from 144 countries to date including sex slaves, murders, pedophiles, criminals, MS 16 gang members, Forencia 14, Trinitaritos, lots of terrorists, tons of drugs, weapons, and stolen goods. You name it. The cartels make billions a week and are in total control."

"You mean corruption."

"No, most Americans are honest. All are demoralized. Why enforce the law when President Brandon and Democrats do not enforce the law? They want open borders and to release all the illegals. No one bothers to look anymore, would you? If they do look, OK, bakshish comes into play. Passage is guaranteed by the cartels."

"Oh my God."

"Illegal is now legal in the United States, as Imam Ali has directed. I will do my part and pay to arm the Jihad. It is my honor."

"This is why you can bring the Ahmad brothers, known terrorists, to the USA?"

"They were terrorists, yes, when they were on the other side, as the best bomb makers on earth. But now they are on our side and they will make bombs to purify the earth, to make things right for Aslan and all the others. They will help make it right, you will see."

"Inish Allah, yes, we shall purify Chicago to the bone."

Ramin told everyone never to repeat any of this to anyone, especially Rashid. "He is too pure to ever know. Like what his name means, Rightly Guided. Do not share any of this with him, ever."

It was agreed.

Rashid rejoined the group and off they went back to Chicago, with Faisil saying, "Now, relax. Listen to the music. We will be home soon and we shall make it paradise on earth for everyone, God willing. Let me drive."

The cabin of the truck erupted in unison, "Allah Akbar, Allah Akbar."

The traffic was light, there were fewer cars with gas prices at $7.99 a gallon. The drive home was faster than coming out. Isn't that the way it always is, wondered Faisil. Better make one quick stop to gas up.

Faisil could see Ramin was awake and he asked, "Can you imagine how stupid this President Brandon is, really? Look at the price of gas at $7.99 a gallon. I can afford it, but really, it is so high."

Faisil went on, "You know he called Saudi Arabia for help. The Prince was to take the call and President Brandon said, no, I want to speak to the real King, your Dad. The Arabs hung up on him. What a fool, they will never forget it."

"Democrats ignore the needy and working people, insult everyone, name call, get involved in war after war and everyone suffers, like Ukraine. They expect the working people to vote for it and pay for it. I wonder who is the idiot in this equation?" He laughed aloud.

He went on, "Ramin, tomorrow I will fly to Pakistan. Drop me off at the airport and keep my truck until I get back. Use it as you like. There's a piece under the seat, a HK P 30 9mm. You never know what can happen when driving a new truck in Chicago. Don't leave it overnight."

"Understood. You leave that soon?"

"Yes. Everything is arranged. I want to see my mother in Lahore too. Is it OK? I will pick you up at 5:00 a.m."

"Inish Allah, you travel safe. I will be outside to await you. I don't have a driver license, but I can drive anything."

"Perfect, no worries, God willing. I will be back in five days. You can pick me up. I will contact you."

"Agreed, my brother, go with God's speed. I will ask Tamara to pack some nice snacks."

"Good idea, thank you, maybe some Medjool Dates. I eat them like popcorn."

"Ok, meet you at 5:00 a.m. in front."

Ramin smiled broadly and hit Faisil on the shoulder. He told him, "My best wishes to mother and God's Blessing unto her and her family."

Chapter 28

By now, Diana's Police Intel group got the vibe. There was going to be a rumble in Chicago, how big she did not know.

During her regular visit with the family, she talked, "Rashid, I am aware something is in the offing. I want to say something."

"Please do."

"Rashid, you are a very special person and you have a wonderful family. When this rumble is all over, you have to think about the future. Without political change everything will go back to the way it was before."

"What do you wish me to do?"

"I want you to register to run for Mayor of Chicago. The deadline is the end of June. I think you will win and I will help you do so."

"I am not even a citizen."

"It does not matter. Chicago now allows aliens, even illegal aliens, and criminals, to run and to vote. You are perfect for the part. Your campaign slogan is simple too."

"I have a slogan? What is mine to be?"

"Making Chicago peaceful and safe for everyone no matter of race, creed, color, religion, ethnic origin, or sexual preference, safe, again."

"That is it?"

"That will win it. I have a feeling this is what you all are working on, right?"

Ramin answered, "Very true. It shall be done, God willing."

"OK, Rashid, tomorrow at 11:00 a.m. at the City Clerk Office, you know the place, I will be there to help in uniform. We will sign you up and get some pictures and press. You are on the way to making life here better. Deal?"

"Deal."

Diana smiled to say goodnight when Ramin raised his hand to speak. "Diana, thank you for everything. You have been an angel to us and Rashid will follow your lead and direction. I want something too."

"What is that, Ramin?"

"As this rumble, as you call it, comes, I will need Intel. If you have it, I want you to share it."

"That can be arranged day by day. You will not go wanting."

"God's blessings to you, Diana. Goodnight."

Diana said goodnight to both men.

Things were going to change.

Rashid asked Ramin what he thought.

"I think God guides you. This woman I admire, she loves you, your family and your children. Do you feel it?"

"Love, well, I still love Aslan. I am a widow. What am I to do?"

"Your heart is big enough, brother, for all that love. Do what you feel is best for your children, for yourself, and for Aslan. She wants the best for her family. You know this to be true."

"How do I know?"

Just then, the rays of the sun, noor, abdul noor – servant of the rays, one of the 99 names of Allah in Islam – burst through the mini blinds with phosphorous white bright light, in an incredibly stunning array.

"There is your answer from the Heavens above. There can be no doubt for you have been messaged from beyond."

Rashid knew it was true. He sat down. He could feel it and it subsumed his entire being. He had been directed.

These men brought their religion and faith with them. They understood how important it was, and they could see the same thing in America.

It was on their money, "In God We Trust."

It was in the Pledge of Allegiance, "One Nation under God."

An it was in the Oaths of Office, "I will well and faithfully discharge the duties of this office on which I am about to enter. So help me God." (Pub. Law 89-554, et al).

It was a moral nation, built upon belief in God, a spiritual nation, yet they could see it disappearing. Erased were the words, Nation and the name of God from the Pledge. There were no more borders. God's name was erased from the Oath of Office. There was no prayer or prayer time in schools. Nothing about God. No respect for one's fellow man. No idea of the divine nature of all human beings made in the image of God.

They knew this to be the doing of the devil, the shytan, and the beginning of the end of the Nation, unless and until they did battle with this devil and destroyed it.

The next day, everyone dressed up in their work clothing, Rashid met Diana at the City Clerk Office and signed off on all the documents. Rashid, being Rashid, already had in hand his own article and byline for the Tribunal to tell the story. As it turned out, the picture that ran on the news and in the paper, somehow, included Diana in the background who was smiling with approval.

She figured she was looking at the next Mayor of Chicago.

Diana and Rashid chatted on the way out of the building.

"I am proud of you, Rashid, so proud. I enjoy visiting with your family and your girls every day. I feel like I am your best friend in the U.S.A. Soon I will have to call you Mr. Mayor."

Rashid realized it was the moment. "Diana, I do not wish you to be my best friend."

"No?"

"In my culture, husbands are never best friends with wives. Each has their own best friends outside of the matrimony. You see, when men and women are in love, it is like an electric wire between them. They are very intense emotions. To add best friends to it, it becomes too much. It burns out the wire."

"Interesting."

"But, true. Men and women, with God's help, can make a new life together. Before that, they create a relationship. This is what we believe, and the man and the woman must care for and nurture the relationship to keep it growing strong. It will be there for them in good and bad times. Make sense?"

"It does. Trust the heart. Value the person, treasure the relationship, I get it."

"So, Diana, we are now in such a relationship, as God has shown me. We are more than best friends. Keep your best friend away from it and we shall grow stronger and closer. Our relationship will be there to support us for the rest of our lives."

"That is so beautiful Rashid. The rest of our lives, you say?"

Rashid smiled broadly, "Yes," as he gave her a hug. "Again, thank you for everything you do for the children. They love you too."

Just as Rashid left, Mayor Heavyhand arrived in the building. She laughed out loud and said, "Nobody can beat my machine, nobody. What a sick joke."

It was not to be a joke, as she would soon see.

Chapter 29

It was time for Faisil's return, certain he had news. Ramin picked him up in his F150. Faisil was all smiles, "We saw the news about Rashid back home. He is a natural for Mayor with his social and language skills and caring heart. Congratulations."

Ramin replied, "Maybe he will win. One thing for sure, we shall win on the battlefield of Chicago, right?"

"Very right, God willing. Everything is arranged as we discussed."

"Thanks to God."

"Ramin, I will drop you off at home. Go to inform Imam Akeem so we can update Imam Ali. I must hurry."

"Agreed. We shall see you tomorrow for the Services at the Mosque. Rashid needs to see you."

"OK, we talk more at that time."

On Friday night, Ramin and his family were bused to the Mosque. His family went inside and Ramin remained outside to have a smoke. He saw, under the street lights, an SUV heading in. It stopped in front of him and a large man got out to open the back door for Gaetano Salvatori to gracefully exit the vehicle, 'dressed to the nines.'

Mr. Salvatori walked straight up to Ramin followed by two soldiers – Rocco on his right and Joey on his left. A 4th man watched over them from the SUV.

"Ramin, my name is Gaetano Salvatori. I am the head of a local organization. This is Rocco and here is Joey." They tipped their heads to Ramin and he nodded back.

"I understand your family has suffered some sadness and I am truly very sorry. If there is anything I can help with, please feel free to say it out loud, OK. We will take care of it. Money or whatever it is you need."

"Thank you, Mr. Salvatori."

"I have information that there is going to be a rumble in the city. My organization never stays neutral. We take sides and we have taken your side. Do you understand?"

"Please explain."

"There is a saying around here about us and how we only kill each other. We know what is bothering you, and we are not involved in those sorts of things. Everything upsets us too. We propose an alliance with you. You leave us alone, and we leave you alone. You give us a heads up when you can. We will share what we know with you. If you need anything, come to us first."

Mr. Salvatori was actually reflecting what Machiavelli said in the year 1500. If two neighbors fight, join the weak one, defeat the strong one and then kill the weak one and take everything. Machiavelli did not make things nice.

That was not Mr. Salvatori's message. He sided with Ramin because he was disgusted with cheap crime in the city which was ruining so many families.

The arson in the city might have been the last draw, as gangs burned down homes and businesses all around town. There were at least a dozen fires 24/7.

Maybe it was the piracy of ships on the lake, who knows. And there was murder, robbery, rape, kidnapping of children for ransom, carjackings, hit and runs, reckless driving, crimes against women, the elderly, students, home invasions, rest home and hospital invasions, business, store, restaurant, office, whole office building invasions, car dealerships, store robbery, extortion, torture, sex trafficking, blackmail, drug crimes, bank robbery, attacks on police stations, court houses, government buildings, jail breaks, dozens killed and wounded daily, any of it – violence constantly increasing and out of control.

If Mr. Salvatori could not take it any longer, no one could. It had to be stopped.

Ramin knew with whom he spoke. He saw the movie. Mr. Salvatori was the real thing. He knew how important alliances were and had no hesitation.

"Mr. Salvatori, we are in alliance. I am Boss here, we agree. We lay off each other and share where we can. Is that it?"

"Yes. Rocco and Joey will come on Fridays at this same time. We will start next week. Tell Faisil. We know him well. Also, I paid Khalil for a whole Halal lamb and all the trimmings, in honor of your brother's late wife. He will bring it to your family and friends or serve it in the restaurant. Whichever way you like for it is the least I can do. Goodnight, Ramin."

Mr. Salvatori turned and walked back to the SUV followed by Rocco and Joey, while the 4th man still watched from the vehicle. It sped off down the street with no lights on.

Ramin had an alliance. Now all he needed was Intel and he knew where to go for it.

During Saturday night's midnight dinner of lobster ravioli in pink sauce, Rocco informed Mr. Salvatori that Ramin put the good word out. Mr. Salvatori smiled. "Good. Joey, take a C note into the kitchen for the crew and tell them that's the best pink sauce since my dear mother's. Rocco, find out when the war starts. I want our people off the streets until I give the message that all is clear."

Chapter 30

Ramin, Rashid, Hamid, Farhad, Faisil, and Abdul all met on Sunday afternoon to make plans. Simple – get the Intel from Diana, the enemy leaders, residency, hide outs, club houses, affiliations, meeting places, rendezvous, drug trading zones, shooting galleries, labs, warehouses, eateries, moles, spies, double agents, and everything possible.

Once the Mujahadeen arrive, bivouac them and their equipment with the various Mosques, going by alpha correlations. On Saturdays, Ramin, would in-person meet with everyone in consolidated groups at ten Mosques, sharing all vital information. All defensive fortifications would be prepared and made fail safe.

Arrival of the Ahmed brothers and supplies would open active recon plus placement of munitions, ambush locations, and battlefield preparation. It would be just like the old days.

With delivery of heavy equipment, arming up, and training, practice could be complete in short order. The Mujahadeen were all experienced thus things could roll. 24/7 patrols would be organized, sniper positions on roof tops and backup. There was a plan for graded response to threat levels from small arms to heavy machine guns, RPGs, grenade launchers, IED, and more. There was provision for preemptive attacks, both inside and outside of the city.

Maps were shared, watches synchronized, and communications secured. The CPD would be treated as an ally, with no harm, in cooperation with Diana and Chief Harlan Struggles out of the public eye. Leaks and compromise would be swiftly and harshly treated.

During the first meeting, comrades in arms teased Rashid about becoming Mayor. By now he was pretty into it. He was a natural-born politician. The worry was all those fake votes pouring in via the unlocked drop boxes set for one man – one vote. As the movie '3,000 Mules' showed, hundreds of stooges stuffed thousands of fake night time ballots into them with no supervision. It was complete corruption. 5,000 votes = $50,000.00. Why not, who cares about integrity of elections?

Some persuasion was required for criminal vote harvesters to refrain from such activities. One sure way was to guard every box and take out any intruder, burn the ballots, and leave him or her there for the next cheater to see.

After a few dozen kills, the ballot stuffers might have second thoughts. If not, they'd die. At the same time, when possible, trail them to the party work places preparing the fake ballots and take them out too.

Rashid thought that was a great idea. "You are the man, Ramin. I may be the next Mayor, you will be my Chief of Security."

"What about me? Hamid needs a role too."

"Press Secretary, you are perfect."

"Faisil, will be my Chief of Staff and Farhad, the Community Outreach Director for Diversity and Inclusion. You have the skills and a pretty face, Abdul, so you with be the Treasurer and count the donations, inish Allah."

"Inish Allah."

Chapter 31

They would use the basement of their Mosque as Command Center with all the communications gear. Next, Diana was invited to share Intel with them on Sunday and she agreed.

At that next meeting, Diana brought everything – organizations, members, hang outs, HQs, labs, warehouses, shooting galleries, rendezvous points, affiliates, home address, main lines of business, rap sheets, maps, cell numbers, emails and identifications for everyone to review.

Over the next week, Mujahadeen began to trickle in. First a few and then many hundreds of them, all fit into the organization as previously planned. The good thing was most had their own transportation and small arms.

Ramin decided that the Mujahadeen had to familiarize themselves not just with various areas but the entire city. They sent scouting operations to scope out everything of interest and then to report back.

Faisil happened to own not one, but two gas stations. They were able to gas up for free as needed. Faisil was doing more than his part.

After two weeks, over 5,000 Mujahadeen were in town, all comfortable encamped and able to meet with Ramin at the main and other Mosque locations as scheduled. The battlefield was taking shape. Scouting, meetings, planning, coordination, command and control were all put into place.

Simple drones with cameras, even for night use, were also enlisted in the effort to free the city of evil. It was one thing to drive around the city by day, but even the Mujahadeen found the city streets, back alleys, abandoned buildings, and docks were blighted and foreboding. Work had to be done.

Pictures were taken of anything that seemed remotely related to the tasks at hand. Everyone shared with Command.

Defenses of all of the Mosques in the event of attack were arranged. Blast walls, fortifications, gun choice and position were all awaiting arrival of the hardware which was coming soon. Nothing was left undone.

By week three, nearly 10,000 Mujahadeen were in the city. The new arrivals were brought up to date. Everyone was in the loop.

Ramin broke the party into 100-man companies within 400-man Battalions to form three full Brigades under his command – 100 Companies / 25 Battalions / three Brigades. One full Brigade was held in reserve for defensive purposes. Each Brigade had its own medic teams. The many doctors at the Mosques supplied the basic medical kits.

Practice and training began in earnest during this period of time. Ramin found his men to be tough, experienced warriors. The weak had not come, only the strong and dedicated.

Imam Ali was kept up to speed. He was thankful and he prayed for God's speed on this important endeavor. He may have been blind but he could see the coming results, the defeat of the shytan, the devil.

Chapter 32

The Ahmed brothers had arrived. Faisil brought them over the Mosque to meet Ramin.

They were twins, Ahmed and Ahmed, no one could tell them apart. They both smoked Camels too. Their trip was good and comfortable they said, except for the border crossing. They had made plans and wanted to get started right away. All the equipment and their special provisions would arrive tomorrow.

Ramin wanted them to get climatized, "Rest now. You can stay here at the Mosque. You won't be seen. Everything will be prepared for you. We start tomorrow. Thank you, brothers, for coming from so far."

"You are most welcome Ramin. We are so happy now to be side by side with you." They both smiled a strange but sincere smile.

As promised the next days were filled with logistics, arriving, unpacking, organizing, distributing, supplies tested for handout, and going live. Training on some newer items took more time than anticipated but all was done before week's end.

Acting as parcel delivery persons, with full beards, the Mujahadeen traveled door to door to all of the marked sites of the enemy. They placed shaped charges in exact locations to achieve maximum internal damage without causing collateral damage – hang outs, meeting areas, labs, warehouses, bars, and the like, all run off telephone calls.

The Ahmed brothers had done a good job.

They had also made and planted dozens more charges around

the Mosques, inside all abandoned buildings surrounding the Mosques, parking lots, and the like. Fortress Mosques.

The plan provided was to divide and rule and cause division within the enemy. The first phase of the plan was set into motion.

One hundred Mujahadeen patrols were sent out on the first night. Drug deals going down, meetings, robberies in progress, fights, meetings in dark alleys, everything that was criminal in nature was destroyed by small arms, automatic fire, grenades, and a few RPGs. A wide area was covered from Calumet to Beverly, Great Crossing, Little Village, Englewoods, South Shore, Garfield, Back of the Yard, Lower Down Town, China Town, West Loop, Morgan Square, Barkley, Downtown, Lakeside, North Point, and more.

Everything came together. The news reported a high level of crime in the streets and for the next five days and nights all sorts of gangs, crime syndicates, criminal organizations, and plain and simple criminals slugged it out in the street, thinking they were fighting each other for territory.

Chief Struggles appeared on TV a few times and had no explanation. He said investigations were ongoing. Sadly to say, bodies were piling up all around the city in big numbers. He also said don't take any street drugs. Everything was mixed up and foul due to the chaos.

The city recovered about twenty bodies a day of people who had to find it out for themselves, mostly Generation Z, not seen by the Chief to be a big loss.

He also spoke to Diane and expected answers but got very little at the outset. She said she would share more once she knew more.

Ramin ordered the move up to the next phase.

The twins were to take out all the marked locations, and save the residences. This was accomplished. There were over 900 fires reported, some out of control which kept the CFD busy for days. No one had any idea of the actual damage or the cause. Gang losses were catastrophic and growing.

At the same time, Ramin sent his two Brigades of Mujahadeen into the nighttime streets and alleys for the next five days to identify targets by search and destroy. He was out in the street himself, every single night, directing the operations. Before dawn, the patrols returned to base to clean up, regroup, prepare defense, and rest for the next duty call.

The TV news reported gang warfare, including out-of-city thugs coming to Chicago to buck up one or another gang. Many were national, even international, like MS 16. To flunk into one of those gangs, members had to kill someone, like a friend, to prove unworthy.

By now, Diana had reported to Chief Struggles that it was gang warfare. New immigrants were involved in reaction to the torment they had suffered, and she advised the CPD to stay out of the way. It was too dangerous and too much heavy stuff going down. Let them kill each other.

Chief Struggles knew there was more to the story. He knew she was somehow involved and knew not to say anything, at least not now. The CPD was ordered to stand down and let the city rock and roll, which it did.

Time for more pressure and phase three.

Ramin ordered the Ahmed brothers to take down all known residences of the gang leaders. Done. More patrols went out after the brief hiatus to hit every gang location, meeting, vehicle, big SUVs, and pepper them.

He sent out pickup trucks loaded with Mujahadeen carrying M240B 7.62 mm machine guns, his favorite CAR 15 M4 Commando rifles, and four of his truck-based M2A .50 Cal heavy machine guns that had been in defensive positions, able to fire nearly 1,000 armor piercing rounds with tracers a minute. A tiny touch of the trigger took down building facades, destroyed any target, and blew up whole cars.

For good measure, he made sure all patrols had RPGs with them just in case they needed more. Snipers were placed on several roofs to keep watch and report street action and to take out the bad guys. By mid-morning, the Mujahadeen were back at base to clean up, pray and eat while awaiting further instructions.

Ramin's drones circled the sky, delivering to him the images he needed to access damage. Fire and smoke obscured some of the view, but overall it wasn't a bad few days of work.

The devils of Chicago were reeling. They knew they were in trouble, and their deeds had come back to haunt them. They knew they would not survive more of this onslaught and kill again.

They called a truce between all criminals. They made a summit. They planned a counter attack.

Defense of a counter attack had been planned from day one. Ramin hoped that it would be the final chapter of evil in Chicago. He had let slip that it was his Mosque that was the HQ and a principal target for the rage of the evil doers. He knew one night soon they would come by the thousands.

Diana got intercepts. He was right, they were coming on the weekend to the Twhead Mosque. He had to be ready. He was so ready.

Diana called Ramin to give him and Rashid her blessings and support.

"Of course, not to worry, this is what we do. Everything will be fine, inish Allah. Please spend time with the family and the children. Diana, you are family too. Thank you."

Diana figured Ramin, this rock of a man, would get it right.

Chapter 33

Mayor Heavyhand had enough. "What's going on, I'm not getting my cash off the street. There is shooting all over the place. I want my money, I want my money. Call the Governor."

"Hello Governor Trickzter, it's Mayor Heavyhand, I need you to get the Guard here now. I have gang warfare and it's got to stop."

"We don't use the Guard to stop gang guys from killing each other. That's not in the Statute."

"Governor, I don't care about the law. I want the Guard."

"Sorry, Mayor, it's not going to happen so deal with it. You are the Mayor."

"Goodbye Governor. Thanks for nothing."

"OK, get me Director Lisa Coma at the FBI, D.C. HQ."

"Hello Director Coma. How are you, it's Mayor Heavyhand."

"Good to hear. Hey, listen, I have a gang war issue here. I need you to send in a couple thousand of your SWAT guys to help out, OK?"

Lisa Coma, "No can do, we don't do gang warfare. Anyways, I have no manpower."

"What do you mean no manpower?"

"Listen, Mayor, we have new priorities, OK. Like I have over 3,000 agents investigating parents who want a say in their children's education. I have another 3,000 agents chasing all over the country after patriots who believe in fair elections and free speech. We call them insurrectionists, and I have another 3,000 agents running cover for the Brandon family. That laptop from hell which I thought we had buried. We are swamped."

"What are you saying, what happened to the law enforcement support?"

"We don't do that anymore. Haven't you notice. We haven't arrested a bank robber or bad guy in months. We're just too busy with new priorities. You are on your own. If you have to call again, please ask for community relations. Thanks and bye."

"Bitch."

"Let's try calling the local office of the FBI."

"Hello, Bud, I need at least 375 SWAT guys on our team to mount an attack on some freaky new gang running the streets on us. We are getting no cash and it's got to stop."

"Yes, I can probably send you SWAT. Who is the target?"

"Twhead Mosque is the HQ."

"I know of it. I will let you know. Maybe we can get the gravy train back on its wheels."

"Please make it quick, I am waiting."

"Sure"

Bud actually had no intention to get involved, not for love or the money, not now.

The Mayor was desperate. She needed street money to make payroll to her own gang. "OK, call the White House, now."

"Hello Mayor Heavyhand. Let me put you through to our Domestic Advisor, Gunter Brandon."

"This is Gunter, how can I help you?"

"This is Mayor Heavyhand. How's things? Hey, listen, I want you to send me the Guard. I have a gang issue in the street and I want the Guard now."

"The Guard, you mean the National Guard. I will have to talk to Daddy. Let's see what the big guy says."

"OK, can I wait on the line?"

"Sure."

"Daddy, I got Mayor Heavyhand on the line. She wants you to approve sending the National Guard to Chicago, now."

"The Guard, what's in it for us?"

"Looks like nothing."

"Come on man, nothing, are you getting soft. I don't do nothing for nobody for nothing, zero. Tell her to get her own damn guard. Is lunch ready? I'm hungry."

"OK, Daddy." Gunter simply hung up.

At the same time, someone else actually had a big idea, way down south in Mexico.

Chopito Loco, cartel leader in Wachatachi, Mexico was getting news from Chicago, but no money.

Something had to be done. He controlled the open border. Why not take over the streets of Chicago and elsewhere too. Go retail, not just wholesale. Even he thought the gangs were out of control.

He called his right-hand man. "Alfonso, get three tractor trailers and heavily armed men to Chicago. Leave tonight and go north as usual through St. Louis into the city. Connect with our counterparts and hit whomever is the enemy. Destroy every last one of them and get my money. Take over the streets."

When Chopito Loco talks things happen. Trucks were rolling north. Diana got the Intel from the AFT. Something was coming north. There were three red Taquatan Beer rigs with Wachatachi plates, loaded for bear.

Diana called a meeting with Ramin at the Mosque and told him what was up.

Ramin figured it would take the trucks traveling on 55 North, along the original Route 66, 18 hours to cross the Des Plaines River north of Springfield. The idea was to intercept and stop the northern movement at the weigh station truck stop located there.

It would take only 4 hours for three pick-up trucks, armed men, weapons, including RPGs, and grenades, to make way for the ambush. The plan was set into motion, with a 14-hour cushion to wait to see the result.

Within the next twenty-four hours the news came in. The trucks were stopped and destroyed by RPGs and a quick blanket of 7.62 mm machine gun fire. A few grenades were placed under the carriages and all was over in less than one minute.

The Mujahadeen were on the way back going 64 miles an hour on cruise control. They would be home in plenty of time for the big finale.

Chopito Loco would not be happy.

Chapter 34

Back at the HCA, the families were all safe. They were ordered to stay in and not leave the apartments for any reason. Not even to put out trash. It was well-guarded by two to four Mujahadeen 24/7.

Somehow the killers in the big yellow sedan, with a damaged front end and broken headlight, figured out that the HCA should be hit. That car, already used in many crimes, rolled into the parking lot just as the Mujahadeen lit up their favorite Camels. Armed men got out of the car and ran toward the stairs to the apartments with intent to kill.

The guards, who were sitting behind the trash bin, put their cigarettes down, opened fire and cut them down. They collected the attackers and put them in the trunk of that yellow beast of a car and parked in on the side road, away from view.

By the time they returned to their chairs, their Camels had only burned half way down. Now that is fast work.

"Do you think more will come?"

"Maybe."

"Good, I was getting bored."

"I am getting hungry."

Ramin would be happy to see that yellow car at a dead stop forever. Yes, very happy. The Mujahadeen had done better than they knew.

Chapter 35

Sure enough, thousands of gang members, criminals, freaks, and the like, converged on the Mosque at 8:00 p.m. on Saturday night. They flooded the parking lots all around the building. Their cars ran up and down the three streets leading into the facility. They blocked all exits to the rear with their vehicles and an unknown number took cover in the abandoned four-story buildings on three sides of the Mosque.

Everyone in the Mosque was heavily armed and ready for a fight to the finish. And, they did.

Gunfire from all sides started the firefight, and it was left to the Mujahadeen to finish it.

Ramin, who was on the roof, gave the command to the Ahmed brothers to take out the buildings and parking lot.

"Take cover," Ahmed called out, while pushing all the buttons.

BOOOOOM!

Deafening explosions made the ground shake. The very parking lot opened up into a crater. The fronts of the buildings collapsed onto themselves and the roofs caved in at the top. The concussion was felt for blocks.

Ramin ordered the grenade launcher on the roof to do three 360s, concentrating most on the rear of the Mosque, and the incoming streets, spitting out over 300 grenades a minute for three minutes.

The six .50 Cal heavies he had were rolled out on their trucks to rake the entire area. Their tracers caused several fires to erupt, all while the Mujahadeen were ordered to fire at will, laying down suppression fire all around the Mosque. At that point there 7.62 mm light machine guns and CAR 15s fired.

Ramin let this go for five full minutes before yelling cease fire. His night vision drones circled overhead, supplying him with visual and heat images. There was not much happening. He ordered his snipers to use their night vision scopes and, if they see anything, shoot.

After a few minutes, it was dead silence. He ordered everyone to stand down, stay in place, and be watchful. This lasted fifteen full minutes. There was nothing, not a sound. Ramin sent out patrols from all of the Mosques to circle the area in search of any bad guys. Sweeps continued throughout the night.

There were a few skirmishes but nothing big. Things were very calm.

Some of the Mujahadeen began to trickle back to their bases knowing it was a job well done.

The battle with the evil doers seemed done.

Ramin called Diana to inform her. She dispatched hundreds of CPD personnel to secure the city. She thanked Ramin and asked about Rashid.

"Rashid is fine," Ramin answered. "He sends hugs and love. He is a very happy man. Let me know if there is anything you need. We are mopping up."

Diane blushed, "Will do."

Ramin was in contact with all the Mosques. They were secure and he ordered defensive forces to remain alert. He sent caravans to patrol the perimeter, to be sure of no more trouble, thus sweeping the city streets clean of any remaining criminal activity.

After a while, Ramin ordered final sweeps of the city and a return to base as things settled down. The CPD in mass took over the task of equal, fair and vigorous law enforcement in Chicago.

At nearly dawn, news helicopters circled overhead. TV was ablaze with images and video. CPD had ordered all divisions of the city into the street for cleanup.

Things were improving by the minute.

Chief Struggles was in front of the cameras, "There has been an unusual event in the city. It appears it is over now and there is an ongoing cleanup and mopping up operation. I have ordered a 12-hour curfew. No one is to be on the street for the next 12-hours. Stay tuned, for your safety and the safety of others. Please stay home. All employers understand that you need not go to work or school. Stay home."

Chief Struggles had every uniform in the street, even those that flew a desk in the station, including Diana. Scattered arrests were being made. Public services and waste disposal joined in to clean the streets. The improvement was unimaginably fast.

Chief Struggles, himself, patrolled the streets. It turned out to be just over eight hours before he called an all clear and things in Chicago got back to a new normal, a peaceful normal.

Chapter 36

Back in Indiana, Imam Ali knew all.

The devil had been vanquished. What the Jihad made in the name of Allah had succeeded. Such satisfaction, thankfulness and bliss.

There was one last man, a fugitive and mass murderer out of St. Louis, who got off a train in the stockyards. He was unaware of the epiphany in Chicago. He smashed a store door in the attempt to rob it but never made it. He was taken apart by a supersonic .50 Cal sniper round fired from a rooftop over 1,500 yards away. He should have stayed on the train.

Imam Ali called a close to the Jihad. There was rejoicing. The Mujahadeen were freed to return to their homes, that included the Ahmed brothers, except they had disappeared into the nation, like invited, deadly guests of the Democrat, open border.

Equipment was ordered and stored in the basements of the many Mosques in Chicago. Some of them he wanted to bring to Indiana as well.

Taking a puff on his water pipe, the Imam wondered, would Detroit, Minneapolis, Milwaukee, New York, Philadelphia, Newark, Baltimore, Providence and Wilmington follow?

He waited for a response.

Chapter 37

Early voting had closed and the unlocked drop boxes were all removed. In person voting was all that was left.

People of Chicago, for the first time, had a real choice. The upstart immigrant had a massive advantage in the polls. There was no fraud to speak of, except for that which might take place in the machine voting. Hundreds of volunteers planned to be present throughout the process.

Diana had done what she said she would do, to run the entire campaign Online with the other ladies of the family via social media. They told voters to watch and listen to the 24/7 sights and sounds of Chicago as it went through its transformation into a peaceful, safe, and beautiful city. It worked.

By the end of election night, the results showed that Rashid had won with an overwhelming 85% of the vote. He would be the next Mayor of Chicago. He did not have a celebration hall or a victory speech.

From in front of the Mosque he made his first remarks.

"Thank you, Chicago, for your confidence. I will not disappoint you. I am already working on new ideas to share with you on my first day. They will surprise and please you as we work together at Making Chicago Safe Again, peaceful and beautiful again, for everybody. Thank you."

Chapter 38

Inauguration Day.

What a day this would be.

Attendees included Governor Trickzter, Mayor Rashid and his wife-to-be, who now was First Assistant Chief Diana and their children Mona and Magi; Ramin who was Head of Security; Tamara and Jamil; Hamid, the Press Secretary, and Yasmine; Police Chief Harlan Struggles and staff; Broderick Simpson – eight year old Spelling B Champion of the City of Chicago and his parents Lavernet and Denziel Simpson; Jennie and her daughter, Amy who was the Winner of the Chicago Children's Science Prize; Farhad and Faisil in their new roles; the Honorable Reverend Luis Tarakhan and his entourage of faithful, dozens of other Moslems and religious groups; and supporters of all races, creeds, colors, national origins, ethnic backgrounds, and sexual preferences, patriots galore, and friends from work, even Gaetano Salvatori, Roco, Joey, and the 4th man.

American Flags and posters about Making Chicago Great Again, and Making America Great Again, were everywhere, and in the corner, none other than President Trump, Melania and Barron, now four inches taller than his Dad.

The only one not present was 44 who too busy to attend, building his $92,000,000.00 mansion on the old Magnum P.I. property in Hawaii. Not bad for someone who was flat broke before becoming President.

Rashid and the whole family were already at City Hall, helping to set up. Diana was organizing some flowers with the others.

Rashid walked over to her and smiled. He asked Diana a question.

"Diana, you are so lovely. Imam Akeem is here now, at my invitation. I would like to get married before I become Mayor. I will have a new, good job, thanks to all of you and to Allah?"

"A proposal, Rashid, is it?"

"Yes, on my knee, before you all."

"Now, you mean?"

"Right now."

"I was hoping for this. The answer is yes."

Everyone jumped with joy. The children hugged Diana like never before. The Imam stepped in to conduct the marriage.

Jennie, Diana's best friend, soon to be Assistant Press Secretary, was chosen to be the Maid of Honor. Magi, Mona, and Amy were the Flower Girls. There were plenty of flowers which were borrowed from the inauguration. Jamil held the ring, the same ring once worn by Rashid's mother.

The CPD Band played the Wedding March and trumpets sounded.

There were hundreds of witnesses in the hall. This was good news. When asked, no one objected.

Getting married is no long ceremony in Islam, it took about eight minutes. The couple was pronounced husband and wife and the bride and groom smiled for pictures.

Hamid, ever resourceful, ordered ten cases of Martinello Sparking Apple Cider. Everyone had some bubbly and three street vendors purveyed Chicago Dogs to the throng all day long. This was Jamil's new favorite food.

Rashid, with Diana at his side, took the microphone. "What do you say, let's get this party started."

Chapter 39

National Anthem was played and everyone stood up.

In the Pledge of Allegiance the words God and Nation reappeared.

Rashid was administered the Oath.

Spiritual morality and patriotism were back.

Police Chief Harlan Struggles spoke first.

"Welcome fellow residents of Chicago. The CPD looks forward to working with the new Administration, hand in glove," smiling at Rashid. "As for the events of the recent weeks, they are under investigation. We do not comment on investigations, so don't ask."

"There is more good news. You know that Captain Diana is now first Assistant Chief of the Department. Diana, as of this morning, with the blessings of Imam Akeem, is now the new First Lady of Chicago. She is the wife of Mayor Rashid, Congratulations. Let's put our hands together for them."

"With the new Mayor's blessing, CPD is now recruiting for 2,500 highly trained, community policing oriented new Officers. There is no longer defunding of the police and no more risk to public safety. The Prosecutor puts the safety of the public at the forefront before allowing any accused person to be released from jail. No one with outstanding warrants, R.O.R.s, pending matters, violations of probation and parole, or on an immigration Detainer, will be released to victimize our people again. This is all good news."

"Our jails are empty, not because we have been releasing arrestees, but because there is no one to arrest. Please understand this – the CPD is back on the streets, in the parks, at the schools, and anyone who commits a crime, rest assured, will do the time."

That brought a thunderous applause.

Diana, who was holding the hands of Magi and Mona, stepped forward to smile, wave and wink at Rashid. She had already arranged, with the help of off duty police, to move from all four of their apartments to the Mayor's Mansion. There would be plenty of room for all of them.

At the same time, Diana made sure to hang a nice picture of Aslan on a Dining Room Wall out of enduring respect for the late mother of her step-children.

She also sent one of her peach cheesecakes and a new Backgammon board for the family. She had already learned the game with the ladies and was getting good at playing it.

Ramin spoke next. "Stop the name calling. It ferments hate. Gen Z was raised on it. You see the result. It creates mass violence. It is killing people and the nation. Show respect, be civil, this is how we must be in Chicago. It must stop, or else."

Ramin walked back to rejoin Tamara, she took his hand, then, his arm, looked up into his face, smiled broadly, and said, "You did well, Ramin, you made it right, thank you."

Ramin smiled, squeezed Tamara's hand, hoping, indeed, things were right in the now revived Chicago.

Next, Mayor Rashid spoke and thanked everyone, then went straight to business.

"Early today, on a xoomy call, I discussed a contribution of $1,600,000,000.00 from our wealthiest residents, corporations and friends. Blofert Riddle has refused. Another call was set for tomorrow. Mr. Riddle suffered a chlorine gas leak at his indoor pool, causing him to cough up a lung and die. Sadly, his champion Persian cat also died. I just got word from the lawyers representing the group that they have canceled the call. They promised to deposit the funds into the City Treasury tomorrow and would try to raise more."

"These monies will be used to fund our Annual Summer Chicago Refresh during which all our teens of 15 years of age and up will report to their school home rooms. They will register and be assigned to summer work including cleaning up, painting and refacing our great City. Each child will receive $8,468.50 upon completion of the work and this will repeat on an annual basis. It is legal, clean and tax free money for honest work."

"The biggest discrimination against our kids is no work and no access to bank accounts. I am pleased to inform you, starting Monday, bankers will be in our schools, opening new savings accounts for every teen. Having legal money in the bank is the best way to prevent criminal conduct."

"This is way past due and I am pleased to get it done."

"This should be going on in every city in America as we are making American safe, peaceful and strong again."

More cheers from the crowd.

"City Environmental Inspectors will walk the streets. Every building receiving updates will be billed and if not paid in 30 days, the bill will become an assessment on the property at 500% interest compounded per day. It will be added to the tax bill until paid. If left unpaid, the City will seize the property. This is a mandatory program to own land."

There were wild cheers. This meant real progress for real people.

"There are two other important people to mention. Broderick Simpson, raise your hand. There he is with his parents. He is an 8-year-old Spelling B Champion and the winner of

$5,000.00 which will go into his trust account. It has already been set up for his beautiful parents, Lavernet and Denziel Simpson. Give them a big hand."

"And little Amy, the daughter of Jennie, please stand up. Amy is the Winner of Chicago Children's Science Prize of $3,000.00 to be put in an account for her. I promise there will be many more such prizes under this Administration for personal accomplishment."

There will no longer be a Democrat Communist stronghold in Chicago. Rashid garnered an unheard of 85% of the vote. It was accomplished all in the absence of those fake votes from the past and the mules and cheats that carried them. It was now a safe place to live, day or night, and in peace, happiness and prosperity with real brotherly love.

Chief Struggles and the CPD, Ramin and the many Mujahadeen that remained, would form the new Community Service Force for peace. They would assure it.

"Now it is time for the Governor to speak."

"You know who I am, Governor Trickzter. We know Rashid and his lovely family. Congratulations Rashid. I have been wrong to my fellow citizens for years. My friend, President Trump, who is standing over there, he is right. My drinking of all the doped up kool aid out of the faculty lounges at eastern Ivy League Schools was stupid. They don't know shit about Illinois."

"People don't want a diet of porn, dope, crime, trafficked sex, handouts, dependency, or a community full of shooting galleries to inject heroin into veins of boys and girls. They don't want sex change operations for kids that don't even know what sex is. They don't want reparations."

"Our people want fundamental fairness, equality, opportunity, respect, and the chance to make something of themselves. That is exactly what Annual Summer Chicago Refresh can and will do, year in and year out. It's a start and it only gets better with time."

"There will be a spiritual awaking in our City, our State, and our Nation. Rashid plans to bring back churches, family, and parental involvement in education which their taxes pay for. God will be in the schools and in our lives. There will be love in our hearts for our brothers and sisters. No more bull shit name calling and cancel culture and any of that crap. What do you say?"

A roar was heard from inside and outside the hall.

"People are sick of negatives and TV propaganda, censorship, mind control, and lies, like President Trump had said."

"They're sick of the Fake News, lies, deceit, concealment by a permanent class of unelected bureaucrats, corrupt officials, crooked candidates, billionaires, foreigners, globalists and extremists, and the controlled media. All these things to sell lies to the public."

"What a sick joke played upon a Nation."

The Governor went on: "Today is a new day. The streets, parks, malls and schools are safe. Our jails are empty and not because of rearrests and release of killers. No. Because we don't have them among the law abiding people anymore. It's like they all left town and are not coming back. At least they better not."

"How many of you ever saw the movie Soylant Green – the ecological dystopian thriller starring the late, great Heston? You should see it, as it and 1984 are pretty telling for us today."

"Why do you think Bill Fakes in Arizona, that fellow Bosk in Nevada, and Gezos in Texas all bought so many square miles of land, and are building 18-foot walls around the properties, with razor wire and lasers, robots guards, to protect it all, with no entry allowed?"

"Well, the answer is they, and others like them, the billionaires, plan on owning the high-tech cities of the future, built for techies and nerds, not us, not you and me, for them, with their own right to collect taxes, form governments, have their own police and fire departments, even renewable utilities, recycling, shopping, schools, and medical care."

"The United States Postal Service will not even be allowed in. No way, all deliveries are left outside the walls, to be taken into the cities by robots. <u>Their own nation within the Nation they abandon</u>."

"That's the plan, and it is happening now, before our eyes, and no one says a word. Private equity has already bought up half the houses in the country. Most of the orchards, the farms, and the meat industry is under attack – they don't want meat either. They say it's bad for the climate, so they are buying up ranches and dairies, not to prosper, but instead to kill all the animals. It is true."

"These people know. If the present policies of the Democrat Socialist Party continue and very soon over 25% of the American Middle Class, 25% of you, will be homeless, broke, hungry, and in a daze 24/7. You'll be eating garbage, maybe each other, all outside those 18-foot walls. The reason being, who today can pay the high cost of rents, food, clothing, energy, gas and insurance?"

"They see it coming, for this City, this State, this Nation, and decent people like you pick up the tab after working for your whole lives. You will be left with nothing, no pension, worthless social security, and a short, violent life."

"President Trump tried to warn us that these enemies of the people, the press, the hi-tech elite, and Democrat Socialists, were shipping our money and jobs abroad. They manipulated the markets, to amass billions, sending our children to fight useless but profitable wars for them, like in the Ukraine. How much did the Brandons make on that one?"

"I just used the word Nation several times. We are a Nation, One Nation Under God with Liberty and Justice for All. Globalist Democratic Socialists don't like the word Nation. They hate borders. That's why 6,000,000 illegal aliens are poring over our southern border, including criminals, thugs and drugs. Who is making money on this?"

"Now, thanks to Rashid, it's different in Chicago. I look forward to working with him to make it different in other great Cities of our State and the Nation. We must all stand up for our Nation, our States, our people, together as one, to fight crime and corruption, and foreign influence, to protect the American way and guarantee freedom, life, liberty, property, education, and equal opportunity for everyone. Otherwise, it's Soylant Green time. What was Soylant Green? Well, it was the sewage of the rich from behind those 18-foot walls. It was treated green for the masses to eat."

"How is that for your children's nutrition?"

"We have all heard about that bullshit "woke." Let me tell you something, Rashid woke me up. He woke us up and this is a different kind of woke which is based upon God and your God-given right to free speech, free press, free association, privacy, freedom to keep and bear arms, and freedom from censorship, from mind and speech control, from spying, and from oppression."

"I feel honored to be invited here. Thank you, Rashid, and my fellow citizens. Let us lock arm-in-arm, all races, all ages, all people, and move on, making this City, this State, and this Nation Great Again."

"Thank you and God bless you."

The earth shook, Governor Governor Trickzter shocked himself.

That was the first but not the last time he would give such a speech on the way, he imagined, to the White House.

At the same time, as a gesture of good faith, he lowered the average room rates in his hotel chain from $550.00 a night to only $400.00 to make them more available to the average joe.

Yeah.

Chapter 40

The next day, the sun rose bright above Chicago. The sky was blue, grass was green, flowers bloomed under the rainbows.

The city was peaceful, happy and safe.

At the same time, a group of self-righteous political party members, activists, and lawyers took off from Washington D.C., headed to Chicago, where they planned to reinstate Mayor Heavyhand and bring litigation.

Ramin was at the airport to greet them.

As it happened, all of the plane's tires ruptured on landing and the plane crashed and burned.

A horrible accident, no words to describe.

Chapter 41

As time passed, people once again strolled in the streets of Chicago, children played in the parks and there was music in the air, even some dancing in the streets.

Chicago was back to normal and people felt safe.

CPD and the remaining Mujahadeen, acting as a community collective, kept the peace. There was a strong presence on the streets, in public transport. Moving stop and check points were utilized around the city, and observation points complimented by closed circuit TV.

Lakes, rivers and land entry points into the city, the airports, bus and train stations, toll booths, weigh stations, and the like, were monitored 24 /7.

Fugitives from the law were arrested and returned to jurisdictions wanting their return.

Criminals with Immigration Detainers were turned over to the Feds. There was no more sanctuary city release of predators into the city.

High School dropout was treated as the juvenile crime. It was truancy. Dropouts were detained, counseled, given an ankle monitor and, where possible, returned home to complete GED education and attend the new Youth Community Services Center. They would get life advice, learn a trade, develop any talent, get a driver license, and get part-time work in one of the Chicago Made Beautiful Programs. They would be working for real money and making the city a better place for everyone to live.

No longer dropout and drop into a gang.

Failure to cooperate in making for a better life for everyone would result in the juvenile being treated as an adult, tried for truancy and contempt, and incarcerated until at least the age of twenty-one. Perhaps, for life, depending on whether or not there were any redeeming qualities to speak of.

A major factor in making all of this work was a simple change in the rules. Juvenile delinquency was civil in nature, not criminal, and the rule in civil proceedings was that the loser paid all court costs. These proceedings, if required, were expensive. Parents would be held to account for and pay the costs out of their expected large annual Tax Refunds. They could afford to pay, but in no way wanted to.

In the past, these parents cheered their children on into crime and gangs, but no more. For the sake of their own pocket book they had a change of heart.

Children had a future, again. They could take advantage of the new youth-oriented city programs, income earning opportunities, banking facilities, hundreds of grants, scholarship, and interest free loan programs to pursue their dreams, for internships, training, sports, entertainment, careers and education.

New partnerships were growing strong between the city, unions, organizations, business and communities assured success for everyone.

Traditional values of God, Country, Family, Life, Freedom, Peace, Security, Safety, Equal Justice, Integrity, Personal Responsibility, Self Esteem, and Respect for one another were back.

Chapter 42

It could only get better.

Yasmin gave birth to the new baby girl, named Aslan.

People, especially young people, had hope, something to look forward to, like never before. Without hope there is nothing but worry, despair and crime.

Rashid, the new immigrants, understood, the most important thing to provide to people was hope. No matter what, there could be no life, no lasting peace, without hope for every single person, for everyone, including all children and adults.

Great good had been achieved in Chicago, everyone could enjoy a life of peace, hope, and brotherly love.

Rashid, however, understood from Diana, he had more to do.

He has to work to protect freedom from destruction via the new Environmental, Societal and Personal Scoring Regime, with its vaccine passport, carbon footprint passport, equity shared property passport, approved consumption passport, energy usage passport, sanctioned travel passport, religious belief passport, approved sexual orientation passport, family size passport, data and news consumption passport, education curriculum passport, no guns passport, no property rights passport, approved entertainment passport, speech passport, federal banking and digital token spending and tracking passport, and the proper life partner passport, all intended to monitor and control every thought, every word, every action of every person, living on either side of that 18-foot wall.

The same Globalists behind fake elections, fake media,

censorship, hate speech, race baiting, constant name calling, division, grooming of children in schools without parental knowledge, chaos, crime, and open borders to tear down the country (yes, they fund it all, provide the employees, share office space around the world with their minions) see this new Regime as the capstone of their quest for total domination.

Even the famous Bob Port himself late to the game, had sifoned off nearly $487,000,000.00 from his own Port's Foundation in the past five years to fund suspect political activities, not what anyone would call charity work. It seems he too had to get in on the action with other billionaire and tech giant, want-to-be dictators.

The plan, obvious to all thinking people, impose it on unsuspecting Americans, ostensibly, to bring back order, all promoted by Democrat Socialist Communists.

Coming soon, except in Chicago, now a safe city in every respect, because Rashid and Diana already asked Ramin, Hamid, Abdul, Faisil, Farhad, the CPD, and his supporters to stand up for freedom.

Chicago would be fine.

Mayor Rashid hoped the rest of the State and Nation got the message before it is too late.

The End

Chicago Jihad
A Fiction Work

Reorder Here:
http://chicagojihad.com

Watch for Chicago Jihad in

Video Game Format, Graphic Novel, Audio and Film